# CATALINA KISS

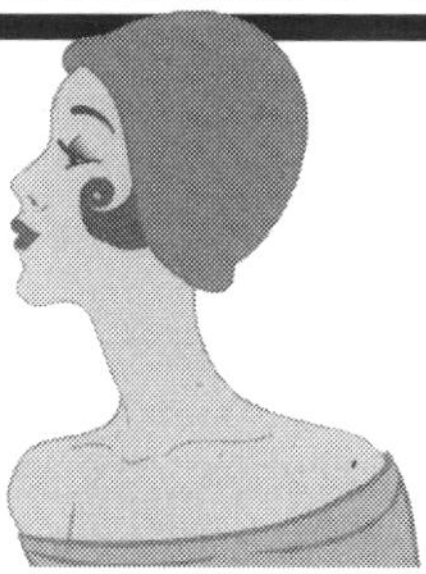

# CATALINA KISS

TRACY EWENS

Montlake Romance

The characters and events portrayed in this book are fictitious. Any similarity to real persons, living or dead, is coincidental and not intended by the author.



Printed in the United States of America.



Published by Montlake Romance

P.O. Box 400818

Las Vegas, NV 89140

ISBN-13: 9781612186603

ISBN-10: 1612186602

*For my Michael,*

*Who cooks for me, makes me laugh every day, and tirelessly teaches me to stop obsessing and enjoy the ride. I love you.*

# CHAPTER ONE

*Birds fly because they know they can.*

*Birds instinctively leave the nest and know they will open their wings and soar without fear of falling. To be a bird*, I thought as we pulled up to the boat terminal. Opening a piece of chewing gum, I used the silver wrapper as a bookmark to hold my place in *The World of Birds* by Samuel Eaton, one of the very first notable ornithologists at the University of California. The pages of the book were yellowed with age and I didn't want to dog-ear a corner for fear of damaging what was going to be a valuable resource.

The door to the car opened as I pulled my glasses down onto my face.

"Miss Ross, what time does your boat depart, ma'am?" Rogers asked, extending his hand to help me out.

"Eight thirty. Could you help me with my trunk?"

"Why don't you give me your other bags and I'll take them all inside for you?"

"No, no, I'm fine with these; I just need an extra hand with the trunk," I explained, closing the door to the car myself.

"Would you like me to check you in at the desk and get you something to drink before your long journey?"

"Rogers, it's only twenty-six miles, and I'm quite capable of checking myself in." I started to once again make a point, but stopped to look at his kind face. The face that dropped me off at kindergarten and the same face that welcomed me home this summer after graduation.

"Thank you, though; it was very thoughtful of you. I'll meet you inside."

Rogers has always been a part of my family, and while I know little or nothing about his personal life, he's a familiar fixture and I love him. There are people that live their entire life and never have even one person looking out for them. I had several, and while most of them were an annoyance during my formative years, I was learning to appreciate them all over again.

The boat terminal hummed with the sound of travelers and families bidding farewell. There was a sense of excitement in the crisp air, as the SS *Catalina* loomed over the scene, barely visible through the early-morning fog. She was a massive steamer ship of glistening white steel. Looking up at her, I stopped to watch the crew prepare for departure. The Wrigleys, the family that also owned the island of Catalina, had built this steamer four years earlier. I was on the maiden voyage with my family the summer before college and in my absence it had become a huge success, pretty much like everything else the Wrigleys touched.

The ship was tied to the pier, which was dwarfed by the size of her stern, with massive twisted lines coiled neatly on the dock like sleeping snakes. She was a beautiful ship, as elegant as a leading lady waiting to kiss her lover good-bye.

I stood by the ticket terminal observing, as if in slow motion, the travelers dressed in their summer finest. Beautiful sheaths and hats, some women with umbrellas to shield them from the sun, and men with light-colored suits and bright summer ties. Everyone seemed ready for an island adventure. Catalina was an escape and the SS *Catalina* was a perfect transport to the island I so longed for.

Since graduating from college I'd felt lost, not that I would ever let anyone know, but something was missing for me. I somehow thought I would emerge from Mount Holyoke a full and complete woman ready to take on the world, but the fact was I hadn't a clue what I was going to do with my life. I had spent so much time fighting what I knew I didn't want that I forgot to figure out what I did want.

I needed time to think, a break from the pressures of Pasadena and the "What will Gwen do with all that education?" discussion. On Catalina, I was enough exactly as I was. Breathing in the sea air, I knew I didn't need to decide anything right now.

I walked up the ramp and into the terminal looking for Rogers, who was of course at the counter checking me in. I wasn't sure why I still bothered protesting.

"Uh-um." I cleared my throat to make sure he knew I was behind him.

"There was a line and you seemed to be lost in a daydream, so I thought—" He stopped and took my ticket from the woman behind the counter.

"Please let me help you, Miss Ross. There are no strings attached, I promise. Just a nice old man making sure you have everything and you get on your boat. No need to write a paper on it," he said with almost a full laugh. I rolled my eyes at him and took the ticket. I was heading over to the snack bar, determined to get my own coffee.

Rogers followed, still laughing. "Remember that, Miss Ross, when you came home for Christmas your freshman year and asked me and Alice to switch jobs for a day so you could gather data for your women's studies project? You were so serious and you must've asked me a million questions. 'What was it like to bear the burden of a housework job?' 'As a man, did I understand now how hard it was for Alice?'" He went on, quite impressed with his memory, and thoroughly enjoying teasing me. It was true; I did use him and Alice, one of our housekeepers, as my subjects for my paper "Men's Aversion to Domestic Work." They were great sports and it was an interesting study, and apparently quite entertaining for Rogers.

"All right, are you quite done?" I said, smiling at him.

"Yes, ma'am. You're such a special girl; I'm sorry—young woman—Miss Ross. You've always been full of spirit and so independent. I love that about you. A take-charge kind of woman, just like my Betty. Now, there was a strong woman. Kept our home and raised my two boys into fine young men. She worked so hard and was a terrific wife. I miss that woman every day of my life." He continued, almost tearing up, "Anyway, Miss Ross, you're like my Betty, full of life and taking nothin' from no one."

I smiled at Rogers and found it odd that he thought me similar to his wife. I didn't remember her; she died when I was young. But from what I'd heard, she was a wife and mother that had never worked outside the home. I was none of those things, nor did I want to be. His wife always seemed much more like my sister, but Rogers was in such good humor, I didn't point out the differences. She seemed to have been a wonderful woman and it was a compliment that I'd brought back her memory.

I took a seat by a terminal window to wait for our boarding call while Rogers stood chatting with one of the crew members. There were brochures for Catalina Island on the table next to me and an announcement stapled to the wall directly above. On the announcement was a picture of a female pirate and a treasure chest with the inscription "Hollywood Island Catalina Is Proud to Announce Our New Casino and Movie Theater Opening Next Year on May 29, 1929."

There was also a sketched drawing of the new casino. It was lovely. I couldn't believe how much the island was growing. Suddenly I felt like a restless child waiting for Christmas. I was restless to see my father and the island, and of course to be a part of the bird park.

The Wrigleys were building a new ballroom, or casino as they were calling it, with a movie theater built specifically for talking motion pictures. Listening to my father tell it, it was unlike anything he'd ever seen: "It's round and appears to jut out from the island coastline like a beautiful diamond solitaire." The old dance hall had been moved to a more remote part of the island and the plan was to turn it into a large aviary as part of the seven-acre bird park. Mr. Wrigley loved birds and he would spare no expense. Father had mentioned it to me while I was still at school and secured an internship for me to work with the bird specialists on the island. I hoped to help them select the species and prepare the habitat for the main aviary. Mother saw it as an opportunity to lure me to the island for the summer.

"Hmm. Ma'am. They're about ready to board," Rogers said, propping open the door with his hand.

"Rogers, when're you going to start calling me Gwen?"

"Probably never, ma'am. You're a beautiful grown woman now, so ma'am seems more appropriate than ever. Are you ready?"

"Yes," I said, gazing out the window of the terminal. "I'm definitely ready."

# CHAPTER TWO

The entrance lobby to the SS *Catalina* was warm in contrast to the cool, white steel of her hull. The smells of newly oiled teak, freshly lit cigarettes, and leather filled the space as passengers made their way to their deck.

I walked past the baggage area bursting with suitcases, hat-boxes, and golf clubs right as the purser closed the huge shell doors. Narrow hallways took passengers past two rows of white wooden lifeboats nested into the side of the ship, in case of an emergency. There were two staircases on the ship, but I preferred the one in the back; it was grander and in the open air. Climbing the stairs past the B Deck, I noticed the beautiful ballroom that took up most of it. The B Deck was completely enclosed in glass and quite unique, especially for a steamer. The last time I was on the *Catalina*, my mother and father danced while I took my brother, map in hand, on a tour of the whole ship. My sister had recently been married, so she was no fun at all. The entire ship was a work of art. Everything about it catered to the well-off tourists dressed up in their best for a passage to an unforgettable place.

"Good morning, Miss Ross," one of the pursers said as I reached the A Deck.

"And to you." I smiled at him, and then found a seat toward the back of the boat, among the sea of perfectly painted white benches.

Just then, the ship's horn bellowed its good-bye to Los Angeles. I stood and joined the other passengers waving to friends and loved ones still onshore. Rogers was standing by the dock, waving as he always did when we went off to Catalina.

The last time I was on this ship was the summer before I left for Mount Holyoke, in 1924, and now here I was again, four years older and—I'd hoped—wiser. The wind off the ocean brushed my face and I looked up to see a huge plume of smoke leave the pipes on the top of the ship. I was on my way.

I walked along the rail, back to my seat, watching the wake of the blue water as the shore moved farther and farther away. Graduating, the internship, medical school all swirled in my head. Medical school was always a dream, but at this moment…I didn't know. So many options, and for the first time I believed my father when he said, "You have your whole life ahead of you." I was Miss Gwendolyn Elizabeth Ross, poised to take on the world, but not quite yet. Something was missing and I was hoping to figure out what it was on Catalina.

A few benches up sat a couple my age, or maybe a little younger. They were holding hands and gazing at each other. My eye was drawn to them because they were not looking out to sea or around the boat at the other passengers. They were looking at each other as if the rest of us didn't even exist. The woman was pretty, but her movements made her so much more. She was graceful, sophisticated, and sultry. Her legs were crossed and she leaned into her companion in an easy and seductive way. He was a handsome man, with his hands entwined in hers. They were chatting about something that was amusing enough for the woman to tousle her hair back in laughter, only to return to his gaze. It was like they were dancing, perfectly in sync. I caught myself staring at them too long and averted my eyes to the other passengers, many of whom were also pieces of artwork.

As I turned to get my book, my reflection in the glass enclosure behind me stared back at me. It revealed auburn hair wrestling free from its clip in the breeze, and rosy cheeks. I was pretty, but not like the woman I'd been admiring. Brushing stray hairs that had finally blown free in the wind, I pursed my lips, still looking at my reflection. *Nope*, that didn't change anything. Still me. Looking put together, classic, responsible, that was easy, but sexy was definitely not in the cards. That was all right. I wanted to be taken seriously, and the world had enough pinups and girlfriend girls. My eyes again drifted back to the dreamy couple, who were still captivated by each other. She placed her hand on his cheek as their lips met softly. The look on her face was electric. I could not take my eyes off them. *What was behind that look?*

For a moment I wanted to escape into her journey. She didn't look serious at all. I imagined that nothing was clanking around in her head. She looked so in love and blissful. Not like my sister's version of love, but genuinely, madly in love. I wondered if you could be a doctor and still look that way. *Was that possible, or did you need to know how to make a perfect soufflé to get that look?*

"Your first time to the island, honey?" a small voice asked from the bench behind me.

"I'm sorry?"

"Catalina...your first time?" She was now making herself comfortable next to me.

"Oh no, ma'am. I spent a lot of time as a child on the island. Beautiful, isn't it?"

"It sure is. So romantic," she said with a nudge to my side.

"I'm sure it can be, but I'm meeting my family. Spending the summer working on the new bird park they're building. Have you—"

"Working? Honey, how old are you?"

"Recently graduated—I'm twenty-four."

"Lemme guess, twenty-four and no beau. Am I right?"

I didn't know what to say. This was a rude question. I shook my head no, feeling slightly embarrassed that I wasn't fit to play the romantic ingenue in this woman's delusion. With that last comment I stood and politely explained that I wanted to sit farther forward on the boat. As I found my new seat, I wondered why strange people always seemed to find me. *As if I wasn't confused enough, now I need a beau…Beau? Who still uses that word?*

The sound of another horn filled the air. The passengers were making their way to the bow and the rail of the boat as Catalina Island came into view. Anyone who has traveled to Catalina knows the boat doesn't actually approach Catalina. The boat is at sea and Santa Catalina reveals herself from the rolling moisture of the ocean.

The breeze touched my face as I walked out to the bow in time to see the first glimpses of Catalina's glorious, rich golden hills. My gaze drifted down the silhouette to the coast. The Saint Catherine Hotel sat on Descanso Beach, as it had the last time I was on the island. The town of Avalon looked as welcoming as ever, children running up the pier and jumping into the water. Memories of my childhood days on this island chased out thoughts of where I was going in my life, who I needed to be as an adult, and worst of all…a beau. I was close to Avalon, and my spirit began to dance in the ocean breeze. I couldn't help but notice the new casino, merely a shell, but nonetheless commanding attention while Avalon and Descanso accepted their positions in the background. My skin soaked up the moisture as the SS *Catalina* pulled up to the dock.

"Throw a coin!" a chorus of voices yelled from the water below.

We were all pressed over the railing and tossing coins into the water as if it were a wishing well. Below, young boys dove in and returned to the surface with their treasures. The passengers on the boat got such a kick out of watching and shouting back at the children. Many of the children even spoke in different accents, like pirates or tribal natives, to entertain their audience from above. As the ship moved into position on the dock, I gathered my things and started to make my way toward the stairs. The crazy matchmaker lady was right behind me again with her brightly colored purse and turquoise sunglasses.

"What's your name, dear?"

"Gwendolyn," I said.

"Gwendolyn, lovely name. My name's Vivian. I hope to see you on the island with stars in your eyes. Don't work too hard," she said with a wink. Then she was gone, down the ramp and into the crowd of arriving passengers.

As I left the boat I noticed a sea of locals and tourists gathered to meet it. *This place is unlike any other in the world*, I thought. If I needed answers to my nagging questions, this was where I'd find them.

It was so good to be back.

# CHAPTER THREE

"Gwennie? Is that you, darlin'?" my father roared from some back room as I walked into the massive entryway of my parents' new home.

The driver was bringing in my trunk when my father came into view. He grabbed me and lifted me off the ground. My father is well over six feet tall, so when he lifts me off the floor—no matter how old I am—I feel two again. My mother followed behind him, with far less enthusiasm.

"Mother," I said, pulling myself together as my father released me from his bear hug.

"Gwendolyn, dear. How was your passage?"

"Great. The casino is magnificent already. Have you been able to walk through it yet?" I asked, looking at both of them with their matching reading glasses hanging around their necks.

"Oh yes, of course. All investors are given weekly tours. Your father and I are invited quite often." Mother used this time to once again reaffirm her status and wealth. Why this affirmation should be necessary for her own daughter was hidden somewhere in the very back of my mother's mind.

"Do you want to go see it, Gwennie?"

"John, let's let her get settled first," Mother pounced, dismissing his excitement.

My mother is a professional enthusiasm destroyer. It has been her specialty my entire life and it's a testament to my father's spirit that she hasn't completely broken him after thirty years of marriage.

My brother once said, "Mom could suck the soul out of the pope." He was right.

"Juan," my mother called to a sharply dressed gentleman I'd never met before. "Please take my daughter's things to her room and instruct Alice to begin her un—"

I interrupted, "Mom, if someone could please just put the bags in my room, I can unpack my own things."

A pause filled the room that seemed like forever as my mother stared at me. She returned her attention to Juan and conceded, "All right. Juan, take the bags to her room. My daughter does everything herself. Not very well, mind you, but she owns it all." She finished with sarcasm, typical for her when she feels the need to take me down a peg or two.

Mother had started already. I had been in the house less than ten minutes and she'd already made me feel inadequate. I was her daughter, not Gwendolyn Ross, nor my father's daughter—*her* daughter. It was all in the way she said things, so condescending and passively cruel. *Not this time*, I thought. *I'm a grown woman, damn it.*

I don't know what came over me. "Juan, is it?" I asked, twirling toward the door.

"Yes, Miss Ross."

"You can call me Gwen," I said, practically jumping into the poor man's lap.

"Miss Ross, I think it's best if—if…" he stammered, looking at my mother.

"All right, fine, Juan, but let me at least help you with these." I grabbed some of my bags and followed Juan up the stairs. I stopped midstaircase and turned to my father. "Father, I'd love to see the casino. Let me put my things away and change. I'll be right down."

I glanced at my mother with as genuine a smile as I could produce. "Good to see you, Mother," I said, making enough eye contact to see her clenched jaw and the daggers she sent me in return.

I reflected on my partial victory as Juan led me down the large hallway. I'd never been in this house and yet somehow it already felt like home. My mother was a master at making her homes feel warm and welcoming. *Maybe that's where she spends all of her kindness,* I thought.

Juan turned a large brass doorknob to a corner room and pushed open a freshly painted white door to what I guessed was my room. The open door revealed a beautiful space filled with a mixture of creams and blues. There was a round table in the corner, near a huge window at the back of the room. On the table were gardenias floating in a crystal bowl. *My favorite. She knows they're my favorite.*

The air filled with their sweet scent as a breeze drifted into my room. It was a sea breeze—there is no better breeze on the planet. This room was exquisite, and I wondered if my mother handpicked everything and put this all together herself, or if she'd barked out the orders before my arrival. For a moment I wanted to believe the former. *She was unable to show her love to me directly, so she used things to love me from afar?* Everything about this room said, "I know you Gwen, and I love you." She wasn't able to say it anywhere else in the house, but behind this big white door she could welcome me and wrap her arms around me.

"Shall I send Alice in, ma'am?" Juan asked politely.

"No, thank you. I'll be fine," I said, running my hand along the bed linens.

"I'll leave you, then. I hope you have a great summer, Miss Ross."

"Thank you, and I apologize if I made you uncomfortable downstairs. You really can call me Gwen, but I didn't mean to disrupt protocol," I said, hoping to counter my earlier image as a troublemaker.

"Not at all, ma'am. I was full of fire once myself," he said with a smile that made me believe him. "Let me know if you need anything." He closed the door behind him.

I fell onto the soft blue duvet covering the queen-size four-poster bed in the center of the room. I was tired and replaying my entrance in my mind. I wondered if I could recall a time with my mother, after the age of six, when I wasn't uncomfortable or faking it. *Why have children if you can't let them plop themselves down on your couch and tell you all about what's going on in their world?* I would no sooner tell my mother about my life than Juan would. Actually, I felt more comfortable with the butler than I did with my own mother. *Mother, were you born this way*? I thought as I put my clothes in the perfectly lined wardrobe.

After about an hour, I descended the staircase, feeling refreshed in my knit skirt and white top. I wore my comfortable shoes, knowing my father would walk me from one end of the island to the other. My mother was in the dining room setting the table for lunch, or rather supervising someone else setting the table. I walked behind her toward the kitchen.

"Will you be joining us?" my mother said, not looking up from her place settings.

"Are we eating before we go into town?" I asked.

"Oh, that's right. I don't know if you're still doing that. Your father's in the study with Charlie Chambers. He's the man you'll be working under at the bird park," she said, motioning toward the giant wood doors off the dining room.

"Oh, I'd love to meet him," I exclaimed.

"Gwendolyn, you can't just barge in there. They're discussing construction issues."

"I think I can keep up. If I'm gonna be part of this, I might as well jump in," I said, moving toward the doors.

"Gwendolyn Elizabeth, stop it!" She raised her voice to an uncomfortable level. I froze.

"Must you always push me?" she asked, now in a strained whisper. "Your father's an important man and he's meeting with another important man. What could you possibly add to that conversation? Wait till they come out and your father will introduce you properly."

I stood looking at her, hoping for some glimmer of sarcasm or indication she was joking. There were no glimmers to be found. *How could she be so…so stupid! Sitting tightly in her little world. Desperately trying to put me in a place that was not only impossible, but would kill my very spirit. As a mother and a woman, how…why did she insist on keeping me a shell of what I could be?*

Intent on not ruining my summer, I took a deep breath, smiled at my mother, and said, "I'm going for a walk in town. Please tell my father if he wishes to join me, I'll be on the promenade." I walked past her as she returned to her place setting. "Enjoy your lunch, Mother."

I burst through the front door, visualizing myself popping the strings of a stifling corset and freeing myself from the tension in that house. As beautiful as my mother and her home were, the way she made me feel was intolerable. To be so defined by your status only as wife and mother terrified me. Those feelings of course made me a leper in my mother's eyes. *It's as if wife and mother are all she needs and the joke is she does neither well. She's a pathetic caricature trapped in a time gone by, when women were accessories—to be seen and not heard.*

I ran down the hill and past the lavish landscaping in front of the house. Different shades of green grasses mixed in with birds-of-paradise, orchids, and irises. The fragrant scent wafted past me on my way into town. Avalon was calling to me.

The hum of the little town was in full force as locals and tourists moved to their choice spots for lunch. Families were heading to Descanso Beach with picnic baskets in hand, while lovers settled into quiet tables for two. The town had grown, but Catalina was always Catalina: a huge green island speckled with little homes, shops, and hillside manors. There are times when I'm on this island that I swear I don't need anything else.

I walked up Crescent Avenue, the main street in Avalon, and watched the children on the beach. When I was a child, I used to run down the long water walk connecting the Saint Catherine Hotel to Avalon and swing under the wood railings to jump into the water. The water is always cold, but so blue and clear.

A few minutes into my walk, I saw the casino poised ahead of me, right between Avalon and Descanso Beach. It was still about eight or nine months from completion, but, even framed, it was unlike anything I'd ever seen—set out from the island and completely round, with the beginnings of a roof. It was a skeleton that grew more and more enormous as I walked. Standing under it, I could see the framework for a massive entry and, with a deep breath, I closed my eyes and imagined it complete. *The elegance that would arrive on opening night. Women dressed in the latest opulent dresses and men in their finest tuxedos.* I wondered who would be playing in the ballroom during the first slow dance. I allowed myself to fantasize about the many dreamy nights this casino would house. The wraparound balcony high above me would be for moonlit strolls and lingering touches. My eyelids grew heavy dreaming, so I took a seat on one of the benches outside the construction area. I laid my head back, allowing the warm sun to flood my face. This place was magical and full of possibilities.

# CHAPTER FOUR

"Chase you from the house, did she?" my father's voice asked from the road behind me. He had a way of saying things that were critical, but not judgmental or insulting. He knows my mother can be unbearable, but his "Chased you from the house, did she?" made it seem not so bad.

"The house isn't big enough for the both of us," I said, smiling over my shoulder.

"Get in, I want to show you something," he said, pushing open the passenger door of his beat-up little truck. My father could afford any car he wanted, and he chose to drive around Catalina in a 1923 Studebaker pickup he bought from one of the locals. He said at the time he loved that the truck was red and yellow. That's my father. I truly love that man.

We drove up past the casino while Father talked about some of the construction delays and the issues they were having with getting supplies to the island. I listened to him go on and on about the island and all the new growth and opportunities. He was beaming, but veering all over the already windy road.

"Dad?" I said as we approached another small truck coming in the opposite direction.

"Hey, I'll bet that's Frank…yeah, it is!" he said, waving with one hand and pulling over onto the small shoulder with the other.

"Frank, headed to the casino?" my father asked, getting out of his truck.

"Sure am, some garbage about running out of pavers? Did you hear about this?" Frank asked, getting out and shaking my father's hand.

"I didn't. There's no way. Remember when they delivered back, what was it, two weeks ago? Those pavers were as tall as a building. There's no way they've gone through them all."

"I'm thinking someone took some for his own patio." They both laughed. Frank glanced over at me as I stepped out of the car.

"You must be Gwen. Your father's been so anxious waitin' on you."

"I am," I said, extending my hand. "That's nice to know," I said, nudging my father.

"You're right, John, she's beautiful." My face flushed and I was instantly insecure. *Comments like, "She's smart, a great gal," I could handle, but "She's beautiful" felt so fake, like they were talking about someone else.*

"I know, inside and out." My father smiled at me.

"You're very kind. Thank you." I regained eye contact. "The casino seems to be coming along nicely, Mr...."

"Sorry, I forgot the formal introductions. Frank, this is my daughter Gwen. Gwen, this is Mr. Cathner."

"Mr. Cathner, it's a pleasure."

"Pleasure is all mine, Gwen. Yeah, the casino's starting to take shape, but I swear those artsy types are gonna be the death of me. Like little prima donnas, they are," he said with a laugh.

Mr. Cathner was good looking, with lovely green eyes peeking through weathered skin. My first impression of him was that he was soft. He had a kind face and looked loved. He didn't have that macho, ax-to-grind look. He had very large hands and a firm handshake. I liked that. I hate it when men shake a woman's hand with some limp version of a man's handshake.

"Easy, Frank. Isn't Michael one of those 'artsy guys'?" my father asked with a smile.

"He is, but he's my kid so I'll forgive him," he said.

"Gwen, Frank's been on the island—"

"Forever," Frank interrupted with a laugh. He smiled at me and paused for a minute, locked on my eyes. "Well, I'll let you two go. I'm going to go let some foreman yell at me and hope he's wrong." With hearty pats on the back, both men returned to their trucks.

"Yeah, Frank…good man…good man," my father said, smiling and closing his door as Frank passed.

"Seems like it. How long have you known him?"

"Well, like he said, he's been here forever. He used to do a lot of construction when the island first got started. Worked directly for Wrigley. Couple years ago, Wrigley opened up the tile-and-pottery factory, so now he runs that. His son does most of the creative work, but Frank keeps the place running," my father continued as he pulled the truck off the shoulder and started up the hill toward the back road of the island.

"I met him a few years ago when we decided to build the house and I got involved with the island's development. His wife passed away a couple of years ago, so it's him and his son. Both of 'em really great men."

We were now up near Chimes Tower, and a great western-style house above the tower that I didn't recognize. We pulled over.

"Have you seen these?" he asked, pointing to the tower and the house.

"That's the Chimes Tower, isn't it? Mother told me Mrs. Wrigley had it built a couple years ago? Donated it to the town?"

"She did, and it chimes every fifteen minutes. Pretty and punctual, but there's just one fly in the ointment." I have never understood that phrase, but it usually preceded a juicy bit of gossip. "You see this pueblo house up the road?" he asked and I nodded. "Well, that house belongs to Zane Grey—"

"The author?" I interrupted.

"Yup, one and the same. Anyway, Grey built this house a couple of years ago before there was a Chimes Tower. Vacation home; he's a huge fisherman. I've had the pleasure of going out with him a couple of times. Interesting man. Intense." I nodded, waiting for why this had anything to do Chimes Tower. "They say Grey and Mrs. Wrigley don't get along. She finds him arrogant and he finds her stuck-up, the usual. So rumor is, to get in his craw, she built her bell tower right here next to his house." Father started to laugh. "She could've put that thing anywhere, but she plopped it right here. So, Grey gets a chime every fifteen, a full song every hour, and there's nothin' he can do about it."

"No!" I said. "Is that really true?" Father smiled at me to confirm. "That's so funny. Did he say anything to her?"

"Not that I know of. He puts up with it. I guess he jokes about it every once in a while, but that's it." We both laughed as Father pulled past the house and continued around the back of Avalon. *Clever, if the story is true. Mrs. Wrigley was definitely my kind of woman.*

"There it is!" he said, turning off the truck. I looked out my window. There were some unfinished stucco buildings and the beginnings of pathways with low, rounded walls. Tucked in the back, barely visible from the truck, was the hollowed-out shell of what used to be the Sugarloaf Casino. The old casino was to be the frame for the new aviary. We were at the bird park site. It was lovely and so quiet compared with the rest of the island. I could hear the sprinklers near the ninth hole of the golf course behind me as I stepped out.

"Damn thing wasn't easy to get over here," Father said, closing the door of the truck behind him.

"It's huge. For some reason I'd pictured it smaller. Wow!" I walked around looking at the octagonal structure, still looking a little frazzled from the transplant to the new space. Father and I walked the entire site. It was about seven acres and a gorgeous spot. The paths and walkways were marked out and some of them had been cleared. It was a maze leading to the habitat areas.

"This bird park is gonna be so fun for you, Gwennie. I was talking to Charlie and he wants you to report here tomorrow morning and get started."

"Terrific! Have they selected any of the birds yet?"

"I don't know. I'm sure they need to finish the buildings first, right?"

"Well, there has to be lead time on getting some of these birds. I can probably get started while they're finishing construction. I'll ask tomorrow." My father looked at me, clearly not sure how to answer.

"I'm so proud of you, honey. You're so damn smart and just as beautiful. I know you don't like to hear it, Gwennie, but you're a looker."

I'm sure I blushed when I said, "Dad, please, let's—" I began walking back toward the truck.

"Get some ice cream?" he interrupted.

"Don't have to ask me twice," I said as we climbed back into the truck.

We drove a little ways back into Avalon and my blushing continued.

"So, how're things on the boy front, or man front, I should say? Anyone I need to worry about?"

"No," I said politely, hoping to end the conversation there.

"No, there's no one, or no one I need to worry about?"

"No to both. I've been really busy, Dad. A few dates here and there, but no one wants to date a woman…a woman with things on her mind." I fumbled to finish my sentence, straining for a change in the subject.

"Sure they do. The right guy likes a woman that's got something going for herself. Times are changing and you…don't overdo it, Gwen."

"What does that mean?" I said, searching his eyes, hoping he wasn't saying what I thought he was saying.

"I mean, don't hide inside your head. Don't be afraid to have a good time. You've nothing to prove, Gwen. You're the first woman in your family to graduate from college. We all know how smart you are, but that's not everything. You have to let people in."

"I let people in," I said a little defensively. "I have friends, I have family."

"Any of these friends guys?"

"No, but I haven't met any worth spending more than a dinner with."

"All I'm sayin' is let yourself feel. Thinking is great, but feeling is what it's really all about." He smiled gently, patting me on the head as if I were ten. We got to Olaf's—they make the best waffle cones on the planet—and we ordered two. My father opted for the triple scoop, with whipped cream and three cherries. We walked along Crescent Avenue eating our ice cream as I tried to understand how such a wonderful man could be married to, well, my mother. My father had such a way of knowing what I needed, even if I didn't know. Whereas my mother…she was, well, my mother. *It must be that opposites attract.* Father and I walked past the aquarium and back to the truck. *I let people in. What's he talking about?*

# CHAPTER FIVE

The birds outside my open window were singing the next morning. Soft morning light filled the room; this was heaven. No noise, only the birds, a cool ocean breeze, and a cozy bed. As I rolled over, I realized it was Monday, the first Monday of my internship. I needed to be on time. Springing into my slippers, I rushed to get ready. I'd not been this excited since my first day of classes in college. There was so much to learn, and this was a real job, where my skills were needed.

I went to the bathroom and splashed water on my face. I took a good look at myself in the mirror. I was well rested and the moisture of the sea air was working wonders on my skin. I felt attractive for the first time in a long while, and I felt needed. This was going to be a hands-on experience, and I knew I would emerge from the internship with some idea of where I was going and what I wanted out of this life. *OK, Gwen, calm down, it's a bird park, not the Holy Grail.*

I got dressed—khaki skirt and a navy top—hair pulled back, and a little lip balm. Being very aware I would be working with all men, I wanted to appear serious, not like a spoiled girl looking for something to do on her summer break. I tied my shoes and took one last look in the mirror. I grabbed my knapsack stocked with paper and books and walked downstairs for breakfast.

Mother was sitting at the table with her usual coffee and dry piece of toast. My father was reading the paper at the other end of the long dining room table. The linens were an ivory paisley print that set off the flower arrangement in the center of the table perfectly.

"Good morning!" I exclaimed, particularly peppy.

"Well, good morning, working girl," my father said, pulling the paper aside to reveal his warm smile. "You ready for the big day?"

"I am and I'm quite excited," I said, sitting in the chair that was the closest to my father without making it obvious I didn't want to sit next to my mother.

"Good morning, dear," my mother said before sipping her coffee. "Alice, please get Gwendolyn some coffee," she said as Alice came through the double doors leading from the kitchen.

"Miss Ross, will you be having eggs?" Alice asked with a warm smile.

"No, thank you, just toast, please," I said, reaching for a piece of Father's paper.

"What time do you need to be at the park?" Mother asked.

"Within the hour," I replied. "I have some time."

"What're you going to wear for your first day?" she asked, leaning back to look at my shoes.

"This is it," I said.

"Oh!" Mother returned her face to the paper, not wanting to start another argument but still wanting to let me know she didn't approve.

"Gwennie, Charlie's a great guy and he really appreciates the help. Keep your eyes and ears open and I'm sure you'll learn a lot," Father said.

"I will. I've so many ideas and I can't wait to get started."

"I know, honey, but you need to let them tell you how they want things, too. They've been workin' on this for a really long time and I'm sure they know what they're doin'."

"OK," I said, feeling odd and as if in a backdoor way my father had asked me to be quiet and follow directions. *These men were in charge, but surely they wanted some input. That's all I was saying.* I let it drop and decided it was time to leave before much else was said. I was in a good mood and wanted to keep it that way. Taking my toast with me, I kissed both my parents and was off.

The site for the bird park was familiar because we'd already walked it, but to see it on a weekday with everyone working was a different experience. There were landscapers, surveyors, and over two dozen construction workers all working in tandem. *This is amazing*, I thought as I walked to the back where several men were gathered.

"Hello there, ma'am," a man with a tool belt greeted me, with a grin that was a mixture of excitement and confusion. "Are you lost?"

"Hi, no. I'm not lost. Could you please tell me where I might find Mr. Charlie Chambers?" I asked, trying to sound like I belonged right where I was.

"Sure." He hesitated. "He's right over there in the red shirt," he said, pointing to a man a little shorter than my father with salt-and-pepper hair. He was dressed nicely and holding a roll of papers in his hand.

"Thank you," I said politely over my shoulder as I walked toward Mr. Chambers.

I could hear the sprinklers turning on for the new patches of grass and the smell of fresh paint filled the air. This was a busy place and I felt my heart jump to be a part of it. I'd also noticed I was the only woman in the area, with the exception of the woman working the counter at the small restaurant near the golf course. She was tending to the coffee and fresh pastries. *It's all right that I'm the only woman*, I thought. *I was invited to this internship and I won't let anything stand in my way.*

"Excuse me, Mr. Chambers?" I asked at the right lull in his conversation with another official-looking man.

"Yeah," he replied, looking at me over reading glasses perched low on his nose.

"I'm Gwen Ross, your intern."

"Yes, Gwen," he said, becoming quite friendly and swiping his glasses off his face. He extended his hand and I felt relieved as we shook hands. "Your father is a very good friend and a downright great man."

"I'd have to agree, sir."

"Well, Gwen, let me see," he said, walking away from the other gentleman. "Oh, I'm glad you're starting today because I do really need your help."

I could barely contain myself. Here I was, walking with the man in charge of everything and he needed my help.

"We need to make a decision on our tile for the aviary and the signs leading up to the bird park. Now, we guys are great at building things, getting ready for these birds, but when it comes to decorating, we're all thumbs," he said with a chuckle. "So, we could use your feminine wiles to help decide on the tile."

He continued in his friendly way, but I felt like the floor was dropping out from under me.

*Did he say "feminine wiles"? This isn't happening.* I was lost in my thoughts as Mr. Chambers kept rambling about things I'm sure I would've found offensive. When I tuned back in, he was giving me directions to the tile factory, where I was to go and pick out the colors of tile for the aviary and the signs. *This really was happening.*

"OK, so when you get there ask for Michael. He'll show you what they have. Use your best judgment on the colors. When it comes to the more technical stuff, like how the signs should read, tell him we'll send over a proof. Don't worry yourself with that right now; we still have some time."

"Mr. Chambers?" I tried to interject.

"Joe, we're not putting that over there," he yelled to one of the workers across the site.

"Mr. Chambers?" I tried again, slightly louder as he was walking away from me.

"Sorry. Yeah, Gwen?"

"I was hoping to assist with selecting the birds and putting together the habitat. I've a lot of experience working with—"

"That's great, but we need to get this tile thing done. Most of the birds are already ordered, so we need to focus on getting this place ready for 'em," he said with a smile, but clearly a little annoyed that I had questioned him. He stared at me anxiously, waiting for me to get on with it and follow his instructions.

"Right," I said. "I'm off, then."

"Great. See you after lunch, Gwen. Good to have you aboard," he said and then he was gone, back into the sea of busy men with important things to do.

I stood there for a moment, taking in what had happened. Four years of college, two summers working for the University of California, honors biology, and still I was, first and foremost, a woman. Good for quaint conversation, fixing snacks, and decorating. *Decorating? You have got to be kidding me.*

As I walked past the golf course on my way to Pebbly Beach, my blood started to boil. I could run circles around most of those men. *What the heck am I doing here? I came all the way home and to this island to pick out tile?* I know that I was sheltered in an all-girls college, but somehow I'd convinced myself that these men would take me seriously. That they would value my education and want my input.

*You're a fool, Gwen.*

I walked through the main entrance of the Catalina Clay Products and Pottery Plant, right up the hill from Pebbly Beach. The jingle bell on the old wooden door attempted to announce my arrival, but there didn't appear to be anyone to greet me. I was fuming, but it wasn't anyone here's fault, so I tried to calm myself.

I walked farther in and found a man, who seemed about my age, in the back behind several boxes. He was looking into a box on the floor and discussing something with an older man next to him. *Perfect,* I thought, *more men!* I couldn't hear the conversation completely, but his voice was deep and he spoke with little effort. *This must be Michael?* He was better looking than I'd imagined. Which was odd, because I'm not sure what I imagined, but he was better. He was tall, with dark, unruly hair that, despite his best efforts to brush it off his face, fell right back into his eyes when he reached into the box. He was wearing rumpled trousers, a sheer white shirt—sleeves rolled—and a sleeveless undershirt. His arms were muscular and tan. OK, his whole body was muscular and tan. His shirt was half tucked in and secured with a brown belt. He was so at ease with himself—comfortable, but not sloppy. It was as if his dress, rather than being dictated by fashion or status, was just organic, a part of him.

His pants and his arms were dusted with reddish powder. I watched the two men discussing...well, I'm sure it was tile. I noticed he didn't have any jewelry on, except a small string of beads around his left wrist. *Nice, it suited him.* I quickly glanced at his hands: no wedding ring and no watch. He removed a piece of tile from the box, swept his hand over the top, and smiled at the man next to him. My pulse jumped; his smile was soft and warm. It woke up his features and seemed natural; this wasn't a family-portrait smile. I was pretty sure I'd never smiled the way he was smiling. It poured out of him like caramel. He ran his fingers through his dark hair and then his deep green eyes looked right at me.

"Can I help you?" He looked surprised to see me.

"I hope so," I said, pulling myself together. "Mr. Chambers sent me to look at tile options for the new aviary. I'm looking for Michael?"

"You found him," he said with that same smile. "Gimme a minute to finish up here and I'll show you what we've got."

"Sure," I casually replied.

My heart was pounding in my chest as I turned to pretend I was looking around. The pounding was because I was in unfamiliar territory. This had happened to me before. It wasn't this guy; it was this situation. I was nervous and angry all at the same time. *What was I doing here? I know nothing about tile or decorating and now I have to talk with another man?* So far, nothing was like I thought it was going to be and...*Stop shaking, Gwen. Get a hold of yourself. The man has paint on his shirt, for crying out loud. Pick out the stupid tile and be done with it.*

I tried to control my breathing to steady my heart. I was angry that I was put in this position, and now I had to pretend I knew what I was doing. *Maybe I should come back...*

"Well, you know my name, and you are...?" Michael asked, coming around the corner, wiping his hands on his pants.

"Gwendolyn...Gwen, I'm Gwen," I managed to mutter, still looking around and avoiding the green eyes. Then I pulled it together, or so I thought. *This guy wasn't going to intimidate me. Damn it, this project wasn't going to scare me.*

"Nice to meet you, Gwen," he said, extending his hand. I shook, and our eyes met. *Firm handshake, warm hands...incredible eyes. Let go, Gwen.*

"Come on over here." He gestured toward the back of the factory and took me into what looked like an artist's studio. He pulled a chain dangling from the ceiling to turn on the lone bulb hanging overhead.

"Excuse the mess. I'd like to say this place doesn't always look like this, but it does," he said with a laugh. I managed a smile. *Of course he seemed nice—he was comfortable with a woman looking at tile. That's where I "belonged," after all.* I started to settle down and focus on the task at hand. If I was here to pick out tile then that's what I needed to do.

"All right, so what are my choices," I said very matter-of-factly, still not looking into his eyes, and trying to appear much more together.

He was right, the place was a mess, but in a really interesting way. There were pictures from magazines pinned up on the walls, swatches of material, and newspapers scattered on a floor covered with water and paint stains. Different tiles, some whole and some broken, hung from shelves and hooks all around the small, cramped space. Nothing was organized, and nothing made sense, but the space was surprisingly relaxing. Total chaos, but comforting. At the end of the room, under a small window, was a large table-desk. Michael pulled three large boards from under the table and put them on top of the mess.

"Here's what we have. We can customize these to a certain point, but I'm pretty limited on my dye colors right now. We're working on some new mixes, but the real vibrant colors won't be an option for a while. We have some soft blues," he said, pointing to the top board. "And this really great yellowish green we finished last week," he added, running his hand along the third tile on the middle board. He was animated and seemed to enjoy showing off his work. "Sorry about the dust, this really gets…yeah." He smiled and then blew his bangs off his face. *Adorable.* "Well, what'd you think?" he asked.

"About the dust or the tile?" I said, quite pleased that my composure and wit were back despite his...well, despite *him*.

"Ha, the tile," he said, looking right at my face with a smile different than the one he gave the older man. This smile was still warm, but it wanted something. This was a teasing smile. I knew in an instant, despite my moment of sharp wit, I was way out of my league.

Layered on top of this little flirtation was the fact that I was backed into a corner; he was looking for a response. He was waiting for an intelligent answer, or a relevant question about the tile. *Tile, tile...what did I think about the tile? I had no idea.*

I was way out of my element, not a good thing for me. Up until this point I'd lived my life quite carefully. If I didn't know something, I learned about it before anyone figured me out. I could feel my frustration and embarrassment. My heart picked up the pace again and it all fell right out of my mouth...

"Well, I think you seem to know a lot about tile, and I know nothing at all. I was sent here by some prehistoric men that seem to think because I'm a woman, decorating is automatically my forte. There's not an artistic bone in my body and, while I could probably draw you a diagram of the chemical compounds found in the clay you're using, that's the extent of both my expertise and, quite frankly, my interest in this little field trip I've been sent on." I took a deep breath and looked toward the floor. I'd unleashed all of my babbling frustration on this poor guy and I was sure he thought I was some kind of lunatic.

"OK," he said with a long pause, glancing at me and again running his fingers through his hair. Then, not missing a beat, he looked down at the boards of tile. "I'd go with this...numbers four and thirty-two for most of the interior walls. They're fairly dark and won't stain easily. I'd use the more decorative tiles like six and eight on the outside of the aviary—they'll complement the existing tile from the old dance hall." He paused for a breath; my eyes were glued to the tile board. "The signs leading to the bird park and the entry sign will be custom designed, so you'll need to ask your dinosaurs what they'd like the signs to say and I'll create a proof for them to review. I'd give it to you, but let me guess, you'll need to leave the proof review to them because you're the little lady?" He looked over at me to catch my eye and finished by staring straight into me. "So, that should do it. Would you like me to give you samples to take back with you?"

"Yes," was my reply. I couldn't take my eyes off him, and, believe me, he knew his performance was impressive. He was funny and not the least bit condescending.

Michael reached in front of me and pulled the lightbulb chain, leaving us in darkness apart from the open door behind me. I turned quickly and moved back into the lighted factory. Michael walked over to several bins up against the back wall of the factory. He gathered four tiles, wrote something in black crayon on the back of each one, put them in a dusty brown bag, and handed them to me. I automatically reached out to take the tile and he placed the bag in my hands, putting his hand on top of mine. His touch was warm, rough, and, despite the constant wiping on his pants, his hands were still chalky and speckled with paint. I stood there, two feet away from him, staring into his eyes.

"Lunch!" A man's voice called from the front door as footsteps came toward us. "Ooh, unless we're interrupting somethin'."

Michael turned toward a short man holding two brown grocery bags and bottles of Coke. They obviously knew each other. Michael helped him put everything on the table. I felt myself backing away when Michael said, "Gwen, I'd like you to meet Hector." I nodded, extending my hand.

"Hector, this is Gwen. She's working for Charlie."

"Lucky Charlie," Hector said under his breath, then took my hand. "*Hola, preciosa*," he said, gently kissing my hand. Normally I'd be repulsed by this behavior, but there was something innocent about Hector's silliness. Before I could say anything, Michael took the now folded-up grocery bag and smacked Hector on the head.

"Cut it out, Casanova!" Michael said with a laugh.

"What? I was just greeting our beautiful guest. Would you like to join us for lunch, Gwen?"

"Oh no, thank you. I really should..." Michael looked at me and my face flushed.

"Let me help you outta here before I have to get out the stick. Hector, say good-bye."

"It was a pleasure, Miss Gwen. Hope to see you around the island," Hector said, smiling from ear to ear.

"Nice meeting you," I said, holding my bag of tile abnormally tight and moving toward the front door.

Michael walked me to the door. For an instant, he placed his hand on my back, guiding me. It was perfectly innocent, but I could tell he felt it was too familiar; he corrected himself. Michael moved naturally and with great ease. He seemed comfortable around women and he had a great sense of humor. I was walking toward the door in a daze of thoughts.

"Gwen," he said at the door.

"Yes," I said snapping my head up, a little scattered. "Um...yes, well, thank you," I said.

"They'll like these tile choices," he said, patting the bag in my hands and smiling at me. "I promise to keep your secret."

"What secret?"

"That you're smarter than they are, of course," he said with a wink.

I smiled back, holding the bag to my chest. "Right, thank you." I walked through the door.

As I stepped out into the afternoon sun, I wasn't sure what had happened, but I knew Michael was someone, or rather some*thing* I'd never encountered before.

# CHAPTER SIX

I stopped in town to grab a sandwich for lunch, which I ate on my way back to the bird park. When I returned Mr. Chambers was nowhere to be found. I asked one of the men on site and was told he left for the day. *Of course he did, perfect!*

I put the bag of tile on his makeshift desk and left for the day, too. It bothered me that I was so insignificant that Mr. Chambers had forgotten he was going to meet me after lunch. It was probably just as well, because I couldn't take one more belittling assignment. There was always tomorrow and the next day and the next...*Great!*

I walked home, feeling defeated and anticipating my mother's "If only you'd not wasted valuable husband-luring years in that school" speech. I'd started the day with such hope and now it looked as though this internship was going to be a series of "female-appropriate" errands. When I got to our front door I said a little prayer that no one would be home.

As I walked quietly past the living room, one of the yellow high-back upholstered chairs swiveled around, revealing my younger brother, Simon.

"What'd they fire you already?"

"Simon!" I yelled, and ran to him for a much-needed hug. "When did you—"

"I got here about an hour ago and was told you wouldn't be back 'til tonight. What happened?"

"Ah, it's a long story and I want to talk about you. How've you been? Stayin' out of trouble?"

"Now, that wouldn't be any fun, would it?" he asked with a crooked smile.

I love my brother. He's always up to something and he drives my parents crazy. I think my father sees a little of himself in him, but would never admit that in mixed company. Father humored Simon and pretended to scold him when he was kicked out of his second private college. Simon shatters my mother's sense of order and, in doing so, makes her shudder at him even more than she shudders at me.

Here he was, sitting in front of me, legs crossed, telling me about his escapades. I droned on about my less-than-exciting senior year. My stories paled in comparison to Simon's. They always had. He was fearless. I told him a little about my awful day at the bird park and he appeared to listen intently.

"You know what you need..." Simon said, teasing me. "A night out with a devilishly handsome man."

"That'd be great, but I don't know any," I said, rolling my eyes. Simon pushed at my shoulder and I punched at his even harder. Years of having a younger brother.

"You're a bull, I need to be careful," he said.

"That's right, watch out," I said, laughing like I was a kid again. My brother was one of the few people who saw the twelve-year-old still living inside of me. He made me laugh like no one else.

"So, how 'bout it? You and me on the town tonight," Simon said, now standing up and dancing around me.

"Simon, I need your help," my mother called from the kitchen.

"Please!" he pleaded, faking a noose around his neck and sticking his tongue out as he walked toward the kitchen, still waiting for an answer.

"How can I resist that charm?" I said, smiling at him. "Now run along and help your mommy."

That evening my parents were sitting on the patio outside the dining room after dinner. Father was smoking his usual cigar and Mother was working away at her needlepoint. Mother's glasses were down, pinching the brim of her nose as she strained to see in the dwindling light.

"Would you like me to turn on the light?" I asked, standing, as I walked out the front door.

"No, no, I'm fine. I don't want to attract the bugs," she said, pulling the needlepoint closer to her small face.

"Karoline, turn on the light, who cares about the damn bugs," Father said.

"I do, that's who. I hate bugs, besides—"

"Gentlemen, lock up your daughters," my brother interrupted, bursting onto the patio in his neatly pressed linen pants and sport coat.

My mother shook her head and my father said, "Just make sure they don't lock *you* up. I don't want to get a call from Bob tonight."

"Aw, don't worry, Dad, I'm goin' out with Gwennie, the good child," he said, nudging me.

"Simon, you could get a nun in trouble," my father said, crossing to him and messing up his perfectly coiffed hair. "But I do love you, son," he said, patting him on the back while my brother repositioned his hair.

"Have fun, too, Gwennie. Have a good time!" he ordered, but in a friendly way. As if I was somehow incapable of having a good time.

"We will. Good night, Mother," I said, feeling sorry once again for my mother because she wasn't part of the fun. She raised her hand to quickly wave good-bye and never looked up from her needlepoint. Simon and I ran down the hill, laughing like schoolkids.

# CHAPTER SEVEN

Antonio's is right on the water in Avalon, with a patio that stretches out over the beach. It's more bar and dance hall than restaurant. Since the Sugarloaf Casino was closed to make room for the new casino, Antonio's has been booming. Simon and I arrived as the band was starting to play. The barmaid directed us to a table tucked in the corner. We had a great view of the band and the couples dancing. The atmosphere made me feel better already, and I was prepared to wash the whole day out of my hair.

Simon ordered us a round of club sodas with lime. I'd been to a few bars in my short adult life, but I'd yet to order an alcoholic drink. Prohibition began when I was in high school, so every alcoholic beverage I'd had since was due to my brother or a friend slipping scotch or gin into a club soda. It's perfectly understood that everyone does it. If we'd been drinking at the house my father would've offered up some of his private stash. He still had reserves stockpiled from 1919, when he first got word alcohol would soon be illegal. It seems silly to me that something so widely used is illegal, but there are a lot of things that don't make sense. It's rumored that we can order alcohol at Antonio's, but Simon felt safer bringing his own.

"So, you glad to be out of school?" he asked, screwing the tiny knob back on his flask.

"You know, I miss it." He shot me an "of course you do" look.

"No, I mean I miss the structure…and the learning. It's easier at school. I had direction," I finished, still trying to figure out what I was trying to say and what I missed so much.

"But you're free. No more homework or damn papers to write. Oh, I forgot I'm talking to the girl who loved all that," he said, nudging me and taking another sip of his drink. "Gwen, how can we be related? If it weren't for your stunning good looks—almost as good as mine—I'd say we're from different families. I mean, look at Mary, she's as dumb as a box of hammers," he said with a laugh.

Mary is my older sister, who married right out of high school. She's beautiful and recently had a perfect little boy, but Simon was right: she's not too bright. She didn't need to be. My mother put her through all the right finishing schools, she's an excellent cook and hostess, and she attracted the right successful man. If you ask my mother, Mary has the perfect life. I love my sister. We're simply different. Mary doesn't understand me like Simon does. Simon sees me as an equal and I love him for it.

As we sat reminiscing, Simon told me of his second expulsion from college and that he wasn't sure about the whole school thing. He said he was thinking of working for our father and I thought that was a great idea. There are some people who don't belong in a school environment and I was sure Simon was one of them. He didn't like the idea of looking for one right answer; he wanted to explore and go on adventures. Father would find him something that suited him and he'd be happier out of school. Simon was so confident and sure of himself. Although he lived in my father's shadow, he wasn't the traditional, overburdened only son. He recognized he was different and reveled in it. I envied him. *He has the luxury of being a free spirit—he's a man.*

As our second round of drinks arrived Antonio's started to fill up; there wasn't an available table in the place. The band was really getting going and at least a dozen couples were warming up the dance floor. Simon's gin was starting to kick in and I felt relaxed. I could feel my face heat up and my shoulders give in. It felt so good.

"So, you gonna tell the bastards off tomorrow, or just do what you're told?" Simon asked, bopping to the music.

"Not sure, probably do what I'm told and hope it gets better. I really want to be a part of this," I replied, raising my voice to be heard over the crowd.

"You pick out the tile yet?" Simon asked.

"Yeah, I went there this morning and left the samples for Mr. Chambers before I left. Did I tell you he didn't even come back from lunch to tell me what my next assignment was? Unbelievable, it's like I'm invisible."

"Gwen, that's how it is, especially with guys Chambers's age. They don't know what to do with you out of the kitchen. Hell, it was just a couple of weeks ago women were allowed to run and swim in the Olympics. It really is garbage, sis. Keep putting yourself in their face; eventually they'll have to take you seriously," he said sincerely, putting his hand on mine. "Look on the bright side, you could be that peacock standing at the bar!" Simon said, referring to a very attractive but very made-up woman in a tight, patterned dress standing near the door. She was in heels that made my feet hurt just looking at them. Platinum hair and ruby lips—she was well taken care of—but the silk scarf around her neck teetered on tacky. Every man in the place had now turned to admire her at least once. She was clearly waiting for someone.

"So, how's everything been at the house? It's gorgeous, isn't it?" Simon asked, pulling my attention back to our conversation.

"Fine so far. You know, Mother is Mother. I can handle her," I said with a smile. "The house is gorgeous, huge, of course. Please tell me you're staying the whole summer."

"You bet!" Simon's eyes wandered back to the woman standing at the bar. "Ah, well, that figures," he said with a snicker, sipping the last of his drink.

I looked over my shoulder; the woman's companion had joined her. He was tall and well put together from what I could see. Then he turned around. I could hear myself screaming, "Look away, Look away," but it was too late. Michael and his hood ornament were looking right at me. He tilted his head to say "Hello" and turned back toward the bar. My face must have been bright red and I felt very warm. *Perfect! There I was staring at him and his date. Really smooth, Gwen.*

"Do you know him?" Simon asked.

"We met this morning at the tile factory. Michael, right?" I said, moving the ice cubes in my glass with my finger.

"Michael Cathner. He's quite the island Romeo. Nice guy, but definitely a ladies' man," he said with a chuckle. "Not that I'm not, but Michael's a pro. He only dates the women vacationing on the island and has a new one on his arm every time I see him."

"Jealous?" I joked.

"Maybe." Simon and I laughed.

"He sure did notice you, Gwen."

"I saw him this morning. I'm sure he's being polite. You said he was a nice guy."

"True, and you're definitely not his type." My heart sank. *What did that mean?* "You're too smart and too together to fall for a guy like Michael, and believe me, he knows it."

"Why are we talking about this, Simon? He said hello."

"I'm only looking out for you, sis. You're a beautiful woman and you need to watch yourself."

"I'm not interested in anyone, least of all the island Romeo. You don't need to worry about me."

The waitress brought over two more club sodas. "Compliments of Mr. Cathner," she said, winking at me. Simon raised his drink and smiled at Michael. I froze in my seat and said nothing. A few minutes later Michael walked by us as he went toward the dining room with his hand on his date's back. My eyes were down, so I saw the hand and her perfect waist, but I didn't look up. I assumed Simon nodded while I tried to figure out what in the world was wrong with me.

# CHAPTER EIGHT

During the next few weeks, the work on the aviary began to show. Some of the surrounding buildings were coming together, too. I was settling into my internship, choosing my battles, refusing to fetch coffee, and occasionally putting in my two cents. I was starting to like working with most of the guys; they would never admit it, but they were starting to see value in working with me.

Charlie agreed to let me teach a clinic to the new incoming caretakers preparing to work in the bird park once it was finished. I'd mentioned that I spent an entire summer during high school working with the California State Fish and Game Commission studying toucans and their habitat. The bird park was set to house at least a dozen toucans. Charlie asked me if I'd be interested in teaching a clinic discussing the challenges the birds would face in a Catalina climate. I wrote my senior thesis on transplanting animals from their native climate, so with a little more research I would feel quite up to the task of helping to educate the staff and, most important, I felt useful and validated. The clinic was in one of the new classrooms in the bird park and the smell of fresh paint filled the room as I entered and prepared my notes.

Toucans are fascinating birds; they would acclimate quite well to the Catalina climate with the help of a mister system and a boost in diet during the summer months. I steadied my nerves, straightened my cards, and turned toward my students finding their seats, all three of them. Three men, that was it? *Well, everyone starts somewhere.* I smiled at the three gentlemen, who seemed more intrigued by the fact that I was a woman than the subject matter. *Deep breath, Gwen.*

Following a brief history of the toucan's native habitat and a silent moment offered up for questions, I launched into the challenges of transporting the birds and the things these caretakers would need to look and prepare for once the birds were on the island. I explained there would be at least a two-month initiation period when things would be touch-and-go for the birds, and they really needed to watch for distress signs and know how to act quickly to remove the birds from danger. I finished up with the daily life and schedule for the birds once the transition was complete and, by that time, my three reluctant students seemed to be actually engaged.

I welled up with pride as I asked one last time for questions and two hands went up. They were real, valid questions, and, following my answers, all three men rose to their feet, shook my hand, and thanked me for the information. I was overjoyed and for the first time in a long time, I was proud of myself. I believed on some small level I'd made a difference. After the men had left I collected my things and glanced to the back of the classroom. Michael had come in and was leaning up against the wall, reading the notes I'd written on the board during the lecture.

"Did you put this lecture together?" he asked, still staring at the board.

"I did; do you have a sudden interest in toucans?" *Steady breath, Gwen.*

"This is really good…interesting."

"You seem surprised."

"I am…I mean, I'm not surprised, but this is really good and your clinic was…" He looked into my eyes and seemed to lose his train of thought. Suddenly Michael didn't look so comfortable, but he continued. "I saw those guys when you first started and I thought you'd be done for, but you really brought them in and by the end they seemed like they learned something. Nice work, instructor," Michael said, seemingly aware he'd been talking a little more than was his norm. He was excited and interested and I didn't think it was because of the toucans.

"Thank you. It felt really good and those guys turned out to be nice. How did you hear the lecture? I didn't see you in the classroom until after they left."

Michael pointed to the two screened windows running the length of the classroom that looked into a courtyard with a new fountain and…newly laid tile.

"Tile…we're doing the tile and I couldn't help…" He seemed embarrassed that he was so intrigued and looked down at my notes.

"So, did you listen to the whole thing through the window?" I asked, feeling confident enough to smile and look into those green eyes.

"I couldn't stop listening. It was really good; I mean, I guess I was a little surprised. A lot of people say they're smart, but, well, it was really good. I came into the classroom because I couldn't see what you were writing on the board."

"The board? You came in to see the board?"

"Yeah, great diagrams?"

"Thanks."

Michael looked at me and seemed uncomfortable, too. "Well, I gotta get back to work. See you around, Gwen," Michael said, leaving the classroom and not making eye contact with me. *Hmmm, maybe my baby browns had a little magic of their own.*

He was the awkward one now, and he looked at me like I was the most interesting woman in the world. He was clearly enamored and that made me really nervous. This was the point where I should intimidate Michael, or he should assume I'm too wrapped up in my work to like men. He wasn't scared; I became more in his eyes. This little flirtation had to stop. It was one thing for my heart to jump when he came into view, but for him to reciprocate? *We're now entering dangerous water.*

# CHAPTER NINE

Charlie let me leave a little early, so I decided to stop for an ice cream at Olaf's. Everyone walking down Crescent Avenue can smell Olaf's, second only to the seawater. I was in a good mood, feeling great about my class, and I wanted a waffle cone. A double scoop of vanilla with a little drizzle of chocolate syrup.

When we were kids my father used to say you could tell a lot about a person by the type of ice cream they chose. "You see," he'd say, "I always order Rocky Road. That means I'm rich, but I'm also surrounded by nuts." Then he'd belly-laugh at himself. It wasn't until we were much older that we even got that joke, but watching my father laugh was about all we needed when we were kids. He told me one day that my vanilla with chocolate syrup showed I was a classic with a little pizzazz.

As I walked out of Olaf's, basking in my memory, I realized that so much of who I was today was because of my father. I always felt special around him, still do. He loved us and made us feel like there was nothing in the world we couldn't do. I reached farther for things in my life because I knew he believed in me. My mother, on the other hand, always grounded us in reality. Now that I'm older I've discovered it was probably a good thing. She'd always tell us exactly how it was, not how it could be, but the cold, hard truth. "Your behind looks big in that skirt," or "You're not the type of girl that can pull that look off," and my personal favorite, "I don't care where you're going to school, if you can't cook, you'll starve," and on and on. Thinking about it now…90 percent of what she said was right, but her delivery always made us want her to be so wrong.

Maybe my mother and father together made the perfect parent, if there was such a thing. Whatever it was, I was feeling pretty good about both of them and myself as I walked home, slowly enjoying the island and my vanilla cone.

Simon came barreling down the stairs as I walked in the front door.

"Hello, hello!" he said in his usual high spirits.

"Well, hello to you. Whatcha up to?"

"Mother and I planted azaleas in the flower bed out back today and I creamed Dad three times in a row at chess."

"Really!" I said, laughing.

"I know, look at me…I'm like the caretaker at an old folks' home. Help, I'm losing my youth."

"No, you really need a night out on the town with a highly intelligent young woman in comfortable shoes."

"Oh boy. Now, that's every man's dream, isn't it?" he asked, rolling his eyes. "But our parents are having the Platts and the Grievers over for cocktails and dinner tonight, so I'll take whatever you're offering. Yeah, how 'bout we go down to Antonio's?"

"Again?"

"Naw, this'll be different, they're doing a beach party cookout sort of thing." Simon pulled a rumpled flyer from his pocket. "A band, lobsters…this looks fun. The Anglers Club is puttin' it on to raise money for some community project they're working on."

"Oh, that's nice, what type of project?"

Simon looked at me like I was a complete misfit for caring. "I don't know, we can find that out when we get there. Come on…it'll be great." He smiled, raising his eyebrows like Groucho Marx. "Or you can pour drinks for the Grievers."

"Antonio's, here we come," I said without missing a beat. "Let me change and you can tell our mother." I smiled.

"Sure, leave the hard stuff to me."

"Tell her it's for charity, that should soften the blow." I laughed as I walked up the stairs.

In my room I washed my face and slipped into a gauzy skirt and some shoes with a little bit of a heel. I was feeling good and anticipating a fun night to cap off my almost perfect day. I washed my face and fluffed my hair. A little rouge and some sheer lip color. I took out the clip that'd been holding my hair off my face all day, letting my bangs hang in a wave across my face. I looked terrific, sun-kissed from my days working at the park and dare I say, a little sexy. I wasn't sure what had gotten into me, but I felt…well, I was certain Michael had something to do with it and tonight I was going to let myself feel this way.

Simon and I arrived at Antonio's; it was packed. The party extended to the small piece of beach below where two bonfires raged. The air smelled of burnt cedar as we walked out back past the band warming up on the patio. The restaurant staff was lighting oil lanterns on sticks all around the beach and on tables as the sun drifted into the ocean. There were even some groups settling in picnic-style, on blankets.

The energy was contagious and I began to sway to the music as we looked around at the growing crowd. Simon brought me a drink and a beautiful woman approached us to talk with Simon. He introduced her to me and said they were friends, but they looked like more than that to me. She kissed him on the cheek and twirled to walk away. Simon stared at her and then turned back to me as if nothing had happened.

"Is she your—"

"Her? No, she's...she's great isn't she?"

"She's certainly beautiful," I said, watching her hook arms with another man standing with his back to us.

He looked older than she was and Simon sheepishly said, "Yeah, well...she's married."

"Married? To him? Isn't he a little old for her?"

"Fifteen years," he said staring at her.

"Older? Good Lord!"

"How do you know her?"

"She was on the island last summer, before they were married." He was sure to clarify. "They were engaged and she was out with her friends. He, he stayed at home a lot, so she and I danced and... we had a lot of fun."

"Simon, she was engaged."

"Yeah, that's a shame, right?"

"You could have gotten caught," I said, sounding like a typical prude sister.

"But we didn't. It was a fun summer and now she's married and I'm sure she's happy."

"Do you love her?"

"Oh, sis." Simon blushed and looked down at the sand. "She's fantastic, but I don't know. She's taken, so what does it matter? He's loaded and I'm..." For a moment he looked so sweet and insecure. "I'm still living with my parents." He laughed with a hint of pain.

"Simon, I'm sorry."

"Oh, come on, stop bringing down the party. Do you want to dance?"

"Dance? Sure, since it's a slow one."

We danced to the thump of the bass and the distant rattle of a snare. The singers had taken a break, so a slow and easy jazz number filled the dance floor set up right on the beach. Simon was an excellent dancer, so I was along for the ride. He could make anyone look graceful. We swayed past the bar and his friend. Simon looked straight into my eyes while she cautiously looked over at us. She was very pretty and very young. Her husband was all buttoned up and didn't look like much fun at all. Of course she was drawn to Simon.

For a moment I saw my brother as a woman might look at him. He was very handsome and very alive. Simon was the type of man whose personality made him even more attractive. I closed my arms around him, putting my chin over his shoulder and giving him a little squeeze as the dance ended. We took a seat on the beach, at a table made out of a barrel and an old ship's wheel.

There was a buffet-style line for the food. Simon and I feasted and chatted with locals and visitors to the island. It was a perfectly wonderful evening.

As the embers began to burn down and the guests began moving up the beach, I went to Antonio's patio to use their outdoor faucet to wash the sand off my feet. Turning it off, I slipped my shoes back on only to look up and see Michael sitting at an outside table on the patio.

A dim, flickering candle lit the side of his face as he looked out over the exiting crowd. I stayed a few steps down on the patio so he wouldn't see me. At that moment, a brunette with a short bob and bare, tan shoulders approached him from behind, wrapped her arms around him, and gently put her lips to his neck. I stayed low as Michael turned around and met her lips with his. She ran her fingers through his hair and they moved into a passionate kiss. Hiding in the shadows, I could hear the crashing waves and see the fires dwindling on the beach. They were nothing compared to the fire right in front of me. Like a moth, I couldn't look away.

This wasn't the same woman he was with the other night. She was different, equally stunning, but different. *How did he do that? How could he have so much passion and intensity for a woman he just met? Maybe they didn't just meet, maybe she was his long-lost love and they were reunited right before my eyes.*

I had no idea what I was thinking, but they looked remarkable together and the kiss...well...I felt it in my knees, so I'm sure she was bowled over. I finally looked away, feeling guilty that I'd intruded on Michael's moment, when Simon came barreling out the back door of Antonio's.

"Gwennie!" he bellowed. "There you are! Ready?"

I wanted to die. *How was I going to pull this one off?* Surely they would be looking right at me when I walked up the three stairs from my hiding place. I took a deep breath and walked toward Simon. Out of the corner of my eye I looked at Michael and his date. They were still enraptured with each other.

I grabbed Simon and we quickly made our way inside. I was almost home free, but I looked back one last time. That's when Michael's eyes opened. Still in midkiss, he looked right at me. *That didn't happen. He didn't just look at me.* At least that's what I told myself as I ran toward the door. *Damn Simon and his big mouth.*

# CHAPTER TEN

The next morning, Charlie and Milt, his chief foreman, went into town for lunch, and I stayed behind to finish cleaning up the aviary, getting it ready for the tile install in the morning. The other buildings were tiled and it was now time to start on the main attraction.

Still nursing a bit of a headache from being at the party last night, I enjoyed the peace and quiet. For a moment I walked around the aviary and remembered it as a dance hall when it was still back in Avalon. When Simon and I were kids we would sneak into town and peek in the side windows, hoping to catch a glimpse of the coolest new dance or some couple holding each other too close. I was never much of a dancer; it always seemed like a passive, typical girl thing to do. Besides, why did the man always lead? But a good slow dance was admittedly, at least to myself, a joy. There's something so elegant about holding another person in your arms and moving in unison. The perfect slow dance should be synchronized, not one leading the other, but leading together. I closed my eyes and swayed with the broom in my hands, drifting for a moment into my own world and that kiss from last night…the moonlight glistening in their hair, that kiss was…

"Uh-um." A person behind me cleared his throat. Even with that slight sound, the voice was familiar. *Please don't let it be him*, I thought, *please, anyone but him.*

"Can I cut in?" Michael said. I could hear the smile, more of a snicker, in his voice.

"Sorry, my dance card is full." I turned toward him, refusing to be embarrassed in his presence one more time. He was smiling and I steadied myself with the broom.

"This place is lookin' good," he said, walking around the aviary.

"We're getting there. Why are you here?" I said curtly.

"Ah, I came to say hello and to drop off the proofs for the signs," he said, surprised by the chill in my voice.

"Charlie and Milt are at lunch. You may be able to catch them in town." I began sweeping again.

"I came to say hello to you, Gwen. I only saw you for a minute last night when you and Simon were leaving." He was being generous. I wanted to scream, "You mean when I was gawking at you kissing that woman?" But I contained myself.

"Oh"—palms sweating now—"yeah, I thought that was you, but we were in such a hurry and you looked...well, occupied," I said. "Frequent that place quite a bit, do you? Different girl every weekend?"

"Not exactly. What's that supposed to mean?" Michael seemed taken aback.

"Well, the first night I saw you at Antonio's I thought you were with a blonde, and then last night—wasn't she a brunette? Different woman, right?"

Michael smiled that smile again. "Are you keeping score?"

"Look, Michael, I know what kind of guy you are. Women are...trophies, collectibles. Tourists, lonely women, no commitments, no hard work, I get it. I appreciate your help with the tile for the aviary and I'm sure you're quite a charmer, but I'm not interested. I'm not the kind of woman you're used to dealing with." My heart was racing by now, clearly betraying my harsh words. "I see right through the sexy artist guy with the beautiful eyes." I was rambling again and he was looking down at the floor, so I stopped. There was a long silence while I put the brooms and brushes away.

"So you think I'm sexy?" he asked, smiling an even more delicious smile.

"Yes!" I wanted to shout, but I wouldn't be another notch on that belt. I looked down and I kept myself busy. I wasn't winning this game. He clearly had the upper hand.

"You know, we could go somewhere and really dance, if you wanted to…no brooms." Michael turned up the corner of his mouth. Clearly my words had not deterred him. Where did he learn this stuff?

"I…don't think that's a good idea."

"What are you so afraid of?" Michael said with a hint of sympathy that really annoyed me.

"Afraid? Oh please, I'm not afraid," I said, rolling my eyes. "What, because I don't want to be paraded around a dance floor like the flavor of the month? No, make that flavor of the night for you." I looked right into his eyes. "I don't dance. Dancing is for… well, it's not for me."

"Gwen, dancing's for everyone. You seemed to be enjoying yourself with the broom there and Simon last night. I'm sure your parents sent you to those fancy finishing schools to learn to dance." He knew he was getting under my skin. *He was watching me last night. How else would he have known I danced with Simon?*

"Oh, I *can* dance. I said I *don't* dance. There's a difference. I'm choosing not to—"

"Have fun? Lighten up? Let your hair down?" Michael interrupted.

"That's right…all of that. I'm not that way," I said, trying to sound convincing. None of this made sense, but I stood tall.

"Hmm. That's a shame. Sad, actually."

"Sad? Believe me, there's nothing sad about me." Now I was angry. "You can't deal with the fact that I'm not fawning all over you and dying to put on the war paint and attach myself to your arm. Two different women in a few weeks and Lord knows how many there've been in between." I was on a roll. *Keep breathing, Gwen, you have him on the ropes.* "Is that how it works, Michael? Do you take these women dancing first and then prance around town telling the guys what 'good girls' they were? No, thank you." I turned to leave, make my dramatic exit.

"Wow, what happened to you? I'm talking about a dance, a night out, and you're acting like I want to enslave you. Gwen, I'm not looking to own you, or any of the women I spend time with for that matter. I want to get to know you. There's a difference. I think you're interesting. You don't need the war paint, no uncomfortable dull conversation, and believe me...no one would ever call you a 'good girl.'"

That last statement shocked me and I was sure that's why he'd said it. My face felt crimson and I was disappointed in myself. All his bull was working and I was attracted to him. He crossed the aviary and touched my shoulder. My breath was gone. No air. I moved quickly away.

"Gwen?" Once he was a safe distance away, I turned to look at him. "You're right that you aren't like any other woman I've met." He paused, allowing his gaze to linger on me. He looked hopeful I could read his mind, somehow know what he was thinking without him having to say the words. "This whole Romeo, island Lothario thing you're putting on me is a little over the top. I've gone on dates, yeah, I like women and most of them are tourists. I live in a tourist spot. I don't form attachments because...well, I didn't want to be tied down...why am I explaining myself?" He looked away and took a deep breath. "Where'd you get this from...your brother? Believe me, that boy's made more indiscretions than I've ever dreamed of." He finished with a laugh, moving closer to me again as my heart began to race even faster.

I didn't trust myself with him. I'd never felt this way before and I couldn't think clearly, which really scared me. I didn't know what he'd do next. My logical mind knew he was a distraction I could not afford. He was the kind of person a girl could imagine spending her life with. That's until the girl gives up everything to cook his meals and raise his kids. I needed to stay away from him, but he brought me closer, pulled me in like the tide. Everything about him was maddening, so at ease with himself, so confident, and definitely dangerous. *I wouldn't do this. Time to finish this up, Gwen.*

"Sure. That's all part of your game right? You're a regular guy and gorgeous women are somehow drawn to you. Please, this is all a game and I'm sure those women are just pieces you move on the board," I said, smiling at him as if we shared an inside joke.

"I like to think I show them a nice time. I'm not hurting anyone—"

"What's that bracelet for…there on your wrist? One bead for every conquest?" That last part was harsh, but I was sure I'd delivered the final blow.

"What? Are you jealous?" I had to give it to him, he kept fighting.

"Jealous of what?"

"Oh, I don't know—sensual women, people having a good time, you name it? What's the big deal? Why come to the island? Stay home! Why's everything so serious?" He was visibly annoyed. "You think too much."

"What?" I was shocked, although I'm not sure why. Of course I thought too much—typical male response. Women are good for several things, but thinking wasn't one of them. I was pretty sure none of the women I'd seen Michael with had the "thinking" problem. Our voices were raised now. "Of course you'd say that; does my brain bother you?"

"No, but your so-sure-of-yourself, judgmental attitude bothers me. You don't even know me. Do you let anyone in, or do you stop and judge everyone at the door?" He bit back and it was a good bite. I felt stupid.

"Are you quite done?" I said, staring at him and wondering how I could've possibly been attracted to such a…

He put the proofs on a box and slammed a rock on top. "Let Charlie and Milt know I need approval on these proofs in the next couple of weeks to start production." He turned to walk away, then stopped.

"You know, it's usually the real smart people, like yourself, that have the most to learn." Then he was gone. I'd won. All that charm didn't work and that's why he was so upset, I told myself. *If I'd been so victorious warding off the enemy, the handsome lover set to ruin my life and rob me of my freedom, then why did I feel so utterly awful?*

# CHAPTER ELEVEN

Days passed and I didn't see Michael. He and some of the other men were installing tile in the actual aviary cage, so I stayed away. Charlie had given me another task, to find the proper heating lamps for the aviary. I was so happy to get an assignment that required some research. I needed something to occupy my mind. I was convinced they gave me the work because they couldn't figure out the wattage themselves.

I spent my time researching habitats and temperatures using Mr. Platt's library and I traveled to the mainland once for more information and some sample lamps. Father drove by the aviary at least once a day and reported the beautiful progress to me at dinner. It seemed Michael was doing a great job and the aviary was looking grand. I asked about Michael without seeming obvious and Father remarked that he had not been himself lately. That he was normally such a carefree kid, but he seemed to have a lot on his mind.

"Probably worried about the aviary and the casino," I said.

"Maybe…but it seems like something more. He may still be getting over his mother. She's only been gone two years and they were really close." I nodded, finishing my dinner. "Have you ever noticed the bracelet he wears?" I shook my head that I hadn't. *Who was I kidding? There wasn't one thing about Michael I hadn't noticed.* "Frank told me Michael made it for his mother when he was eight.

She wore it every day, right up until she passed away. He wears it now to feel close to her. Kind of sweet," Father said.

The room began to spin. He made it for his mother? He wears it to be closer to her? I felt like my chest was going to cave in. *What kind of a person is so mean? How could I have said it was made up of a bead for each of his conquests? Why didn't he say something? What would he say? "You're a cold, heartless, emotionally messed-up woman." That would be appropriate.* I felt horrible. I'd definitely scared him off for good. I was sure he thought I was an awful person and my heart ached a little at that thought. *What's wrong with me?*

The next morning, I walked into town intent on finding a great cup of coffee and some time alone. I still felt horrible about what I'd said to Michael, but I was determined to get over it. It was Friday and Avalon began bustling with newcomers when the morning ship arrived. I stopped with the other locals and welcomed the ship, and then sat at Joe's Café for a cup of coffee. As I looked through the finger-smudged window of my booth, I was thinking about Michael. I'd only seen him a handful of times, but we were so explosive around each other. He filled me with such mixed emotions, all of them intense and...alive. I'd come to Catalina for myself, to answer my own questions, and now I found myself distracted by this man. I'd been cruel about the bracelet, there was no denying it, but I hadn't known. More important, I was sure I'd scared him off at the aviary by exposing him for what he truly was, a womanizer—a good one, but one nonetheless.

Finishing up my coffee and paying my bill, I decided to walk over and look at the casino, finally. Michael was working on the aviary tile, so I wouldn't run into him. I wasn't sure how I was going to face him after our last argument. I rounded the corner by the drugstore and walked toward Sugarloaf Bookstore. As I continued, *damn it!* There he was, sitting alone, drinking coffee, and reading a book outside Sugarloaf. I tried to change my course without looking silly, but it was too late to cross to the other side. He looked up at me as I passed.

"Gwen?" he asked in a rich and smoldering morning voice.

"Michael, how've you been?" I tried to seem unfazed, as if I'd simply run into anyone. My heart was pounding.

"I'm doing well, thanks for asking. You haven't been to the bird park in a few days. Did I scare you off? I mean, with my fierce womanizer vibe?" He smiled an "I have the upper hand" smile.

"No, not quite." I laughed. "Charlie has me working on this heating project and I've been away. I hear the aviary is going very well."

"Yeah, it's…you should come by and see it, but you sound busy with what you're working on, so…" He looked down, marking his page.

"I'll be there next week. Why aren't you there today?" I said, looking ahead to the casino.

"The grout's setting, so I have the morning off." An awkward pause filled the space between us. "Yeah…so, where're you off to?" he finally said.

"Oh, I'm out taking a walk to…the casino."

"Have you been inside yet?"

"Not yet, my father keeps promising to take me in, but he hasn't had the chance."

"I'm only sittin' here and my coffee's cold." There it was, that smile. "Would you like me to take you through it?"

I would, more than anything. It was so good to see him, but I'd already broken the tie. My nasty comments the other day sent him a clear message that I wasn't his type of woman. It was best to leave well enough alone.

"No, thank you," I said, looking anywhere but at his face. "I'm going to look around the outside right now."

"OK...yeah, there isn't much of the inside to see yet anyway. Probably bore you. Maybe some other time?" He sounded deflated.

"Sure. Michael, I wanted to tell you that I'm sorry about..." *Find the words. Come on, Gwen.* "I'm sorry about the other day. I should not have argued with you. It's really none of my business. You've been helpful with the tile and..." My response was pathetic, but I desperately wanted him to know I was a human being. I hadn't meant to say hurtful things about his mother. I needed to stay away from him. We couldn't be friends, but there was no harm in apologizing.

"It was more like sparring. No harm done." Again with the smile. Then he looked up, crossed his legs, and effortlessly said, "Arguments, as you put it, should be your specialty. Don't you think?" I looked at him with a blank stare. *What are you talking about?* "You study chemistry," he continued. "So you should know all about why we argued."

I blushed and laughed, "Yeah, I've studied chemistry, but biology was my major." *Who cares, Gwen? He's flirting with you again and you're giving him your curriculum?*

"Even better!" he said, quite pleased with himself. "Certain things are drawn to other things, right? Properties, or whatever... like magnets. Take my mother and father, they couldn't have been more different, but they had chemistry, a fire that drew them together against all odds." He was looking right at me and I was right back where I started. "What seems logical is not always the answer, right? Opposites attract? Chemistry, or biology...powerful stuff, right?"

*Yeah, but my major wasn't chemistry...Did he say a fire that draws people together? Where does he come up with these things? We have chemistry? I mean, I know he has chemistry, but I have chemistry?*

I said nothing. I nodded, considering his idea, as if it were logical. He clearly knew nothing about chemistry or biology, but he was trying to make his "opposites attract" point and that was incredibly...*Wow!*

"That's an interesting point. I've got to get going," I finally said, gesturing good-bye.

Michael opened his book again and read out loud: "Thou art to me a delicious torment."

"Sorry?" I said, trying to hold it together. He made it really difficult to walk away.

"Ralph Waldo Emerson...he knew a thing or two about fighting or chemistry...whatever you want to call it." His cheeks were pinched with red. He seemed to catch himself. Michael was attempting to tie science and literature together all in an effort to explain why we didn't get along. He was flustered and so was I. It was time for me to leave.

"I really should be going," I said, trying to be polite, but I'm sure I came across as distant and cold once again.

"Sure...didn't mean to scare you off. I'm not quite sure what the hell I was saying. I'm babbling." Running his fingers through his hair with a deep breath he said, "I enjoy our arguments, Gwen, so there's no need for an apology." He smiled, collected himself, and stood with his book tucked under his arm. "So, I'll see you around."

"Sure...yeah...yes, I'll see you." I fumbled and then turned to leave. *Well, I don't think that was an argument,* I thought as I walked away. *So...should I turn and see if he's looking at me? Straight ahead, Gwen, he's quite finished with you for the day.*

I walked over to the casino construction site and changed my mind. I didn't want to see the casino. I couldn't think straight. My conversation with Michael, while cryptic, was enchanting and he grew more and more interesting. He was not intimidated by my studies; as a matter of fact, he brought them up often. He was unlike any man I'd ever met before. "I enjoy our arguments," he'd said. *Was that meant to be a sister-brother teasing thing, or was there more?* I found myself thinking about this until I realized I was on my way back home. I'd been walking deep in thought, replaying every gesture and piece of conversation, hoping to uncover proof of what I'd already suspected. Michael liked me. He found me interesting. *Gwen, you and every other girl on the island.* I woke myself up and realized I was falling for it, again. Falling for his charms and games. It was time to refocus. I needed something else to think about; I needed a project other than my limited work at the bird park. *Maybe I should write an article for the local paper? I'd look into that,* I thought as I climbed the stairs to the house.

When I walked through the door, my mother was buzzing around the house, more animated than usual.

"Gwen, I'm glad you're home. Mrs. Platt sent word she would like to speak with you, sort of a 'welcome to the island' thing. She'd like you to join her for tea at four today. Her house is up the road. Do you remember? You should have plenty of time to change. You're going to change, aren't you?"

"Yes, Mother, I remember and...I'll change. That was nice of her. Just the two of us?"

"Yes, your father took your brother to the Tuna Club this afternoon. Your sister and George will be arriving on the evening ship, so I want to make sure everything is ready." She stood dusting the leaves on the plant by the door. *Where did she learn that this needed to be done?*

"Go upstairs and then get along to Mrs. Platt. Please be on time."

I walked up to my room. This was going to be what I needed. Tea with Mrs. Platt, the two of us discussing real-world things. *Maybe I should write an article about her for the paper,* I thought as I turned on the bathtub faucet.

# CHAPTER TWELVE

Mrs. Platt's house was magnificent and very opulent, even for an island home. It was twice the size of our house and three stories. It hung over Avalon and the harbor like a rare and priceless chandelier. Mr. Platt built it for his wife when they first came to the island back in 1912. The house was white with dark green shutters and modest columns at the front entryway. There were football fields of grass in front of the house and a large, circular driveway. Rose bushes, probably fifteen of them, caught my eye as I approached the door, surrounded by planters filled with exotic plants.

The Platts were wealthy, but very down-to-earth, especially when they were on the island. Mr. Platt smoked cigars on our porch with my father and they argued over which team was going all the way to the World Series. My mother was in awe of Mrs. Platt, I imagined solely because of her wealth and status. Mother felt everything she did paled in comparison to Mrs. Platt. I didn't think Mrs. Platt even cared to engage in a rivalry. She was like the girls in school for whom everything always appeared to work out. She was attractive and elegant, always appropriate and the perfect hostess. With her age came this great wisdom and people were drawn to her.

I rang the doorbell and was greeted by the high-pitched bark of their little Pekingese dog, Stella, as their maid opened the front door.

"Miss Gwen, my how you've grown. A beautiful young woman now," she said, holding Stella in her arms.

"Thank you, Margaret. How are you? It's been such a long time."

"Good. You know, living on this beautiful island…How could things be bad?" she asked with a smile. "I'll let Mrs. Platt know you're here. Why don't you go into the parlor?"

"Sure. Good to see you."

"You too, Miss Gwen."

I walked through the double doors of the parlor, closed them behind me, and took a seat at a table near the corner bay windows. The entire room was filled with sunlight and the most incredible view of the ocean I'd ever seen. I'd been in this room a few times as a child when my parents were invited for tea, but never alone. I was a little intimidated and intrigued at the same time. The room was decorated with roses and rose patterns. The couch was soft, with an oversized slipcover and large pillows on either end. There were white, floor-to-ceiling bookshelves on the wall behind the couch. Beautiful Tiffany floor lamps sat on either side of the couch. Mrs. Platt was an avid reader, but she read what my father called "girly" books. Romance and poetry were her favorites, and you could tell by looking at her collection: tales of unrequited love and smoldering passion, not exactly the types of books we were encouraged to read at Mount Holyoke.

"Gwendolyn Ross!" Mrs. Platt exclaimed, bubbling into the room through the double doors like a film star.

"Mrs. Platt," I said as I began walking toward her outstretched arms for a hug. Mrs. Platt wasn't a tall woman. She was round, full, and always dressed like she stepped out of a catalog.

"Ah, let me look at you," she said, holding me by both shoulders. "My, how you've grown, dear. You're gorgeous, and, I've heard from your father, quite accomplished."

"Well, he does love to brag."

She smiled. "Oh, still so humble. Did you enjoy school?"

"Yes, very much. I actually miss it."

"Come, let's sit." She sat on the flowered couch facing the window and gestured for me to sit next to her. I sat looking out the picture window that overlooked all of Catalina.

"So, our Gwendolyn a graduate from one of the Seven Sisters. We're so proud."

"Thank you. How'd you know about the Seven Sisters?"

"Dear, those colleges are creating new frontiers for women. Wellesley, Vassar, your school, it's very exciting. Women are finally being given an opportunity to receive a man's education. According to Mr. Platt, some give an even better one. It's incredible to see in my lifetime."

"It's an amazing school and it transformed the way I see the world. Anything is possible, but—"

"But, what?" she asked, surprised.

"Well, it's one thing to be in a school environment, sheltered from the world as it really is. I just thought…Oh, I don't know what I thought."

"You thought an education would give you all the answers? Sweetheart, there's still a life to figure out. Education or no education, life's still an adventure and a royal pain sometimes. But you… you've been given a foot up. Just knowing there's more, a career, public service…such a gift."

"I know, but what good is the gift if out in the real world no one takes me seriously? I can't—"

"Gwen, things take time. You're young, so this is hard for you to grasp, but there've been so many women before you who knew they'd never see in their lifetime a woman going to college, let alone graduating. You stand on so many of those women's shoulders. Don't complain, dear. Your road is much smoother. My entire life,

I've had to learn anything of interest in private, by swiping my husband's paper once he was done. Always in secret," she said, pouring another cup of tea. "You can learn out in the open and are respected for that education—you mustn't complain."

"Did you enjoy being a wife and mother? What you're describing sounds sad. Has your life been awful?"

"Oh no, dear, I love my life. I get immense pleasure being James's wife and mother to our children. I keep a fine home and we've surrounded ourselves with wonderful friends. I want for nothing. You've different opportunities, that's all I'm saying. At the same time, I must say that even if I'd achieved higher education, I still think my marriage and children would be as prized to me as any book."

"Really? Or do you think that's because you didn't have exposure to other things?"

Mrs. Platt seemed a little taken aback by my bold question, but she kindly replied, "Gwendolyn, there're things you can't learn in a book. Things that only life can teach you. Loving and being loved are great gifts. Using your mind is a wonderful gift, too, so I suppose a mixture of the two would be ideal."

"I suppose, but that balance sure seems difficult—"

"Aren't you full of difficulties for such a young woman," she interrupted. "Go get what you want. You know what you'd love? And it'd be so good for you, too." Mrs. Platt tapped her chin and then went on at some length about the eagle habitat tucked back in the interior of the island.

She explained how two of the eagles had recently had an egg hatch, and that I should see the wonder of this little bird family. She said she would arrange to have a guide take me into the interior and show me the habitat. It would take an entire day. I ended my visit with Mrs. Platt very excited. I agreed to meet back at her house in the morning. She'd arrange the guide. She was pleased, and, walking me to the door, she said this trip was exactly the thing I needed. I wasn't sure why seeing an eagle was exactly the thing I needed, but I was grateful for the adventure.

That evening my sister, Mary, and her husband, George, arrived with their new baby. Mother was the most animated around her first grandchild I'd ever seen her. Mary and George looked exhausted and seemed quite eager to hand little Stephen over to Mother for the evening. Mother and Alice took turns cooing while Mary and George enjoyed adult conversation and listening to Simon's adventures.

Sitting at the table, I looked at my sister and brother differently than I had before. We were all getting older, starting families, or, in Simon's case, avoiding becoming an adult. It occurred to me that I was right in the middle of Mary and Simon, literally in age and figuratively in life. I still questioned things and had uncertainties like Simon, but there was a part of me that wanted some answers and a sense of being settled, like Mary. I was on the cusp of making choices and I didn't want to make the wrong ones. My father says mistakes are inevitable, but I'm not comfortable with that notion.

Dinner was delicious and the whole family seemed to work that night. Simon and I played cards with George while my parents sat with Mary and the baby. All was right with the Ross family. No carousing with Simon, just quiet time at home. I turned in and drifted off to sleep thinking about the adventure into the interior Mrs. Platt had waiting for me.

The next morning I arrived at the Platts' as planned. I walked toward the door, still waking up. Mrs. Platt, chipper as ever, walked out her front door with a young, good-looking gentleman wearing a large-brimmed hat. She was carrying what looked like a picnic in a bag. As the two of them approached, I lost my breath… again. Michael…Michael's face was under the large-brimmed hat.

*Breathe, Gwen, it's really important to breathe!* I put on my best fake smile.

"Good morning, dear." Mrs. Platt reached out and, giving me a hug, she whispered, "You'll thank me for this."

Patting me on the back, she gestured to Michael, who was standing beside her and clearly just as surprised to see me.

"Gwendolyn Ross, this is Michael Cathner. He's agreed to take you into the interior of the island. He's a pro and knows everything there is to know about our little island."

"I think you may be talking me up just a bit. Gwen and I have already met, ma'am."

"Oh?" Mrs. Platt was playing a game.

"Yes." I finally spoke. "On a few occasions. Michael, it's nice to see you again."

As if things were not uncomfortable enough, Mrs. Platt then said, "Well, all right, then. You two are already off to a great start. There's a delicious lunch in the knapsack. Enjoy yourselves!"

While I didn't look directly at him, as we got into the truck I was certain Michael was uneasy, too. Not nearly at my level of discomfort, but we were clearly witnessing Mrs. Platt's matchmaking skills. We both waved good-bye.

"I didn't know you were the friend Mrs. Platt wanted me to show around the interior," Michael said almost immediately.

"I could see you were surprised. I was equally to find out you were my guide."

"I can take you home if—"

"Oh, you don't want to go? If you need to be—"

"No, that's not it, I…don't want you to feel…uncomfortable."

*Uncomfortable, why did he think I was uncomfortable? He couldn't see my hands sweating. Did I look uncomfortable? I was fine. There was no reason to be uncomfortable. I wanted to see the eagles and he knew about the island. Mrs. Platt was right. This was a perfect situation. I could handle this, and, besides, there was no place on the planet I wanted to be more than sitting right next to this man.*

"I'm not uncomfortable at all. Thank you for taking me. I'm very excited to see the eagles."

Michael smiled, eyes still on the road, "OK then, great." We pulled up to a gate obscured by bushes and vines. Michael explained that the rest of our trip would have to be on foot.

"Are you sure you're up for this?" Michael asked, coming around to open the truck door for me.

"Are *you* up for it?" I snipped, accepting his hand as I got out of the truck. *Are you flirting, Gwen?*

"Yeah, but I've done this trip a few times."

*Oh, please, how hard could this really be? We're walking.* I wondered if the "man of the island" routine had been tried on other women, or if this was the real Michael. Either way, the outdoors agreed with him.

"I'll be fine, thank you."

# CHAPTER THIRTEEN

We passed through the gate and into the interior of the island. The town of Avalon began to disappear. Michael walked the path ahead of me, glancing back to make sure I wasn't far behind. He was a beautiful man and today I was definitely seeing him in his element. Nature agreed with him and, with each glance over his shoulder, I hoped he saw that it agreed with me, too. That I looked as glistening and energized as he did.

"You all right? Is this too much?"

"No, I'm fine. It's so…incredible back here," I said. It really was breathtaking and his concern for my well-being was no longer annoying. It seemed genuine and not some commentary on my being the "weaker sex."

"Isn't it amazing? This is where the magic is," he said, absolutely glowing. "You know there're so many people that never see this side of the island. I really can't imagine that."

"Do you hike back here a lot?" I asked.

"I used to with my father before I left for college, but I've not been back since I returned to the island. My mother…" He stopped.

"Your mother?"

Taking a deep breath. "Well, she loved it back here, too."

"My father mentioned your mother passed away. I'm sorry."

"She did, it was a couple of years ago now and...well, we miss her." He trailed off and I could tell he was uneasy, emotional talking about his mother. Michael closed his eyes as we walked and turned his face into the breeze as it passed. He looked like a child experiencing nature for the first time. I could tell he was thinking about his mother and all the suave rogue charm melted away. It was only for a few seconds, but so true.

"What did you study at school?" I said, trying to move off the subject.

"Business," he said, opening his eyes.

"Really? I don't mean to be surprised, but you don't seem..." *What're you trying to say, Gwen?*

"Yeah, well, I was trying to better myself. I had big dreams." There was the hundred-watt smile again.

"You don't have big dreams now?"

"Ah, well, it's a little complicated. You see...Yeah...does it seem like we're talkin' a lot about me? You're next," he said, playfully pointing at me. "Anyway, my girlfriend at the time left me for my best friend during our senior year of college. I spent four years trying to be something I wasn't. Sitting in classes that bored me to tears, convincing myself this was what it meant to be an adult. This was how a guy landed the career and the girl." Michael stopped talking and turned to me on the trail. "She held my hand across the table and told me. You know somewhere in my mind...I knew...I knew it was over, but do you know what my first thought was?" Michael ran his fingers through his hair, looking down at his boots. He was blushing.

"What?" I said quickly, as if I was waiting for the plot twist in a good movie.

"I did all this crap for her and now she's leaving me? Isn't that crazy?" Michael laughed and started walking again. I continued to follow, completely engrossed in our conversation. I'd never seen this side of him before.

"I blamed her for everything and came back to the island with a really big chip on my shoulder. My best friend, the guy she left me for, was loaded and successful. Aw, hell, I just wanted to read and recite poetry; I was never gonna be a businessman. She wanted more and now that I look back on it, I don't blame her. I gave up and came back where I belong. Pathetic, right?"

"No, I don't think it's pathetic. You, you're perfect…uh… perfectly suited for this environment. Your work's inspiring and besides, what girl doesn't like a guy who recites poetry?" I was trying to make him feel comfortable. Our eyes met. Michael smiled politely and looked away. *Gwen, whatever you're doing, stop.*

We walked through the newly cleared trail for miles. The wind tickled the trees above, turning itself into a gentle breeze that cooled our faces. I closed my eyes and looked up toward the trees as Michael had before. He was right, this place was magical, and the farther we trekked into the interior of the island the freer I felt. Away from town, my family, and the pressure, the questions, I felt free to be me. So much of my life felt like dodging comments or insults or judgments. Here, I was relaxed, and it dawned on me how rare a feeling that was for me. Then I opened my mouth.

"Have you ever been in love?" *Jesus, Gwen, where did that come from?*

"Excuse me?" Michael continued walking, but slowed down to walk beside me. There was no turning back now. He heard me, but he wanted to hear me ask again.

"Have you ever been in love?"

"Um." He paused for what seemed like an eternity. "I thought I was, but when it was over I knew I wasn't. I told myself I was in love with the girl I was talking about before, but you can't be faking it when you're in love, right? And I had no idea what love was." He looked at me, appearing a little awkward himself, smiled, and looked at the ground ahead.

"Do you know what love is now?" flew out of my mouth. I wasn't sure where all of this was coming from, but I felt like talking, apparently about love.

"Gwen, are you doing some kind of research on human emotions now?"

He was mocking me and I must have blushed when I said, "Forget it."

"No. I'm sorry. I didn't mean to insult you. I'm sure you talk about love…Crap, I'm sorry. Love, let's see, no, I don't think I know what love is. I know how other people describe it, I read it in poems and stories, but I'm not sure if it really exists like that. If it does, it has definitely not happened to me." He looked at me with what appeared to be sincerity. "You?"

"Have I ever been in love?" I said, looking around at everything.

"Yeah."

"No."

"That's it, just no?" he asked.

"I answered the question, didn't I? I've never been in love," I replied, feeling a rush and pressure fill my body. The real world returning, standards, judgments, they were all back. *Why had I brought this up? Maybe I was studying human emotions.*

"OK, do you know what you're looking for?" Michael asked carefully.

"I'm not looking for anything." The defenses were back up. I was in dangerous water and way too comfortable around him. *Time to quash that.* "I've never understood that about women. What're they looking for? What if what you're looking for never shows up? Then I guess you settle because you've convinced yourself you should be in love and having children by now? No, thank you. I'm not looking for anything I can't get myself. I'm looking to experience my life. I want to travel more and read more and do more of this."

"This?" Michael looked at me.

"Yes, walking until my feet are sore, breathing in the fresh air, connecting with what's real in this world besides the party dresses and using the correct fork. Being here with you has been the best part of my summer so far…" I caught myself, and my face burned again. I was staring out at the trees and I didn't dare look at him. I kept walking and it was silent for a moment.

"Me too, Gwen. Me too."

# CHAPTER FOURTEEN

Michael clearly sensed my discomfort and changed the subject. "So, why birds? Why're you so interested in birds?"

"Well," I said, gradually making eye contact again, "I've always been fascinated with flying. When I was young my father told me stories of the Wright brothers and da Vinci's flying machines. I was glued to his stories and, as I got older, I had more questions. I wanted to understand the science of flying. So, my father bought me a bird, a parakeet actually, and then a parrot, and, before I knew it, I was studying the wild birds around our house and I fell deeper and deeper…" I stopped. "I'm rambling, sorry."

Michael was staring at me with a look I had never seen before, "No, you're not rambling. I'm interested. Did you major in…um, birds in school?" He laughed at himself.

"Ornithology…the study of birds was my minor. I majored in biological sciences."

"Really? I didn't think there was a big draw for women in science," he said, stopping again on the trail.

"There isn't. I went to Mount Holyoke and there were only four of us in the department."

"Hmm, so why science?"

"That's easy. You gather data and that leads you to a logical answer, proof. I like the certainty, but there's still so much to learn.

It's an exciting area. I'll probably go to medical school. OK, now we're talking way too much about me."

"So, you need an answer? Does it matter how you get there? What about the journey while you're gathering the data?"

"Gathering data is pretty exact. There're proper procedures that must be followed, controls that must be established. I'm not sure what you mean."

"The journey. I like the journey and I'm not sure we ever really know the answer. I'm sure that's why I like stories and poems. You probably hated essay questions in school," he said, laughing and holding a branch back for me as we walked.

"Hated them. Ah, I hated English, too. Why can't they get on with it? It's a door and the man walked through it. Why is that a whole chapter? And Shakespeare? Ahhh!"

Michael was laughing, too, and told me how he wasn't great at science, but did like physics. He explained that a business major was all wrong for him and economics almost killed him. Brushing his hair off his forehead, he looked at me, as we both now stopped on the trail to drink some water.

"See, opposites, it's so weird how different we are and..." His eyes drifted as he moved closer, until he was directly in front of me. I could feel his breath on my face. I didn't say a word. He leaned over to my ear. I could smell his mixture of sweat and dirt and something else that made his scent irresistible.

"Stand still," he whispered, as his hand came up past my cheek.

*Oh my!* I was completely paralyzed. I stared into his eyes, noticing for the first time there were little flecks of brown...Michael cupped his hand and pulled something from my hair. It was then I realized this wasn't a romantic moment, but something was in my hair. I backed away quickly.

"What? What?" I exclaimed, shaking myself and running my fingers through my hair. I'm sure I looked very attractive, like I was having some type of seizure.

"Calm down, Gwen," Michael said, now cupping something in his hands. "A butterfly. It got caught in your hair. I didn't want you to start swatting at it. It's nothing to be afraid of."

"Oh." I collected myself and walked over to look. Michael's hands parted; a blue-and-yellow butterfly sat there, not knowing if it wanted to leave, and then flew away.

"Beautiful," I said.

"Definitely," Michael replied, looking right at me. I looked down, brushing my hands on my pants.

Michael jogged up a little ways. "We're here, or as close as they'll let us get."

"Who're 'they'?"

"The eagles, of course," Michael explained as we moved close to a ravine. The eagles were nesting in a large eucalyptus. With binoculars we were able to see them up close. Michael laid out a blanket and we sat for hours watching the mother eagle, and occasionally the father, tend to their chick. Eagles are massive birds with wise faces. They knew we were there the whole time and they tolerated us. They were swooping and diving to their own choreographed dance. The mother and father were equally powerful. They gathered food, raised and protected their nest, all side by side.

Michael was able to pry the binoculars out of my hands long enough for us to have the lunch Mrs. Platt sent. It was delicious and I was having the best day. Michael and I talked and laughed. He was intelligent and funny. I'd never realized life could be this way, with or without a man. He made me feel free and comfortable in my own skin. We were doing something most people never did, watching these magnificent birds, and we were two people enjoying the day. Not a man and a woman, just people, side by side. *Incredible.*

We packed up our things and began heading back. It would take us a couple of hours to get to the truck and we needed to be out of the interior before sunset.

Walking for almost an hour, soaking up the day, and being in the same space with each other was a feeling I couldn't describe. I'd never felt this comfortable with anyone.

"So what's it like doing the tile for the casino? It's so huge!" I asked as we walked.

"It's really a larger project and there're so many people involved. Right now they're upset because we don't have the really vibrant colors they're looking for to do the outside entrance murals. They're thinking they'll have to complete the entry with painted murals and then come back in later, once we have the tile, and go over the pictures. My father is really frustrated and he's working really hard to get me what I want…I mean get them what they want."

"Who're they, the designers?"

"Yeah, it's one thing to design something in your mind—that's a creative process. It's another thing to have the materials to see it come to life. That's the more practical part and when the two conflict it can get pretty ugly."

"I bet. What are the murals for the entrance going to be?" I asked.

"It's a whole under-the-sea motif. The side panels are sea creatures and underwater scenes. The center panel right over the box office is going to be a big image of Poseidon with his trident…you know, god of the sea? It's really going to be sensational, if I can get the colors we need."

"Oh…well, that sounds like it'll be nice," I said, less enthusiastic.

We walked for several minutes before Michael said, "What?"

"Nothing. It figures they'd put Poseidon as the main focal point," I said, blurting out my opinion again.

"You've got something against Poseidon?" Michael asked, still smiling.

"No. I—it's nothing."

"Gwen?"

"It's always a man. Men are building the casino and the bird park. Men run the world." I tried to tone down my annoyance, but I was right. "Men have all the power, so it seems appropriate that even in art, who represents strength and power over the sea and who is guarding the new and glorious casino? A man. Women get to be naked statues, seductresses, and the prows of ships. It's just typical." I took a breath.

"Well, you have *The Birth of Venus.*" Michael was trying to figure out if I knew what he was talking about. "Botticelli?" he playfully questioned.

"I know what *The Birth of Venus* is." Now I was annoyed.

"Sorry. Gwen, the casino is a big deal and Poseidon *is* the god of the sea." He looked at my face, hoping for some understanding. "Things weren't simply handed to men, you know. We've worked to settle countries and build industry. Hell, we're responsible for making this country the great land that—"

"Really?" I interrupted, feeling the anger bubble over.

"Yeah, really," Michael snapped back.

"And women had nothing to do with that?"

"I'm not saying that. The support of women is very important and men couldn't do what they do without it, but at the end of the day men are getting things done."

"Yeah, because they make sure women aren't allowed to do anything," I said, raising my voice.

"Maybe that's the way women want it. Not everyone's like you, Gwen. In fact, I've never met anyone like you. Most women want to sit in their drawing rooms and have someone take care of them. The only women I know that work do it because they have to. You're—"

"A misfit? Michael, women are dying to be heard and taken seriously. The women you're talking about do those things because that's all they know. Everyone, by nature, wants to be validated. I can't believe you could be so…" I stopped.

"So what?" he had to ask.

"Stupid!" There it was, I blurted it out and I could tell he was shocked.

In retreat, Michael fell back on sarcasm of his own. "Oh, I'm sorry, instructor."

"See? There you go mocking me about teaching that clinic when you said you were impressed. It's ingrained in you. Men!" I wanted to run away. The day was taking a turn and this suddenly felt awful.

"Well, I may be stupid, but I do know a thing or two about women and—"

"I'm sure you do!" I had to get that in.

"And most of them are dull, shallow, and content being draped in ornaments from their rich husbands. I'm not saying you're a misfit, but you are definitely not the normal woman, Gwen."

After a long pause, we went back through the gate as the sun set behind us.

"Michael, this has been enlightening," I said, extending my hand to shake his. "Thank you so much for your keen insights."

Shaking my hand he said, "Gwen, you're getting all upset over nothing. I was telling you how it is, or how I see it. I didn't mean… At least let me drive you back home."

"Please don't. I understand. Thank you for a lovely day and… yeah, good-bye, Michael." With that I turned and walked away.

"Don't you want me to…" I heard him say as I left him in the distance.

I was angry. Angry with myself for thinking Michael might be different, angry that I had had such an incredible day that ended in yet another argument, and so angry with him and his stupid, stupid comments. My anger soon turned to sadness as I entertained the idea that maybe I *was* a misfit. Why did I get so upset? To a certain extent he was right. Most women don't want anything more than what they have, but there are so many women that want more. I argued with myself. *What were all the questions about being in love? Why was I letting him have this effect on me?* It was dark now as I approached the house. My entire body was sore from walking. *I was not a misfit and I wouldn't be treated…Lord, I've exhausted myself,* I thought as I entered my parents' home and crawled up the stairs to my room.

# CHAPTER FIFTEEN

Morning peeked through my window early. Simon was knocking on my door.

"Gwen? Wake up. Can I come in?" he asked, sounding like a toddler.

"Yeah. What is it? Come in," I said, clearing my throat.

"Happy Saturday! How would you like to go sailing?" he asked, smiling and moving his eyebrows up and down.

"Sailing? When? What boat?"

"Well, before I left home to come here I bought a new thirty-seven-foot Nevis from these up-and-coming boat makers, Sparkman and Stephens. Sparkman's dad went to school with our dad and now his son and this other guy make boats. The one I got was the third boat they've made. It'll be a collector's item—these guys are going to be huge. Anyway, I didn't think it would be ready until after summer, but they called yesterday morning to tell me it was done. While you were hiking all over God knows where yesterday, my friends Robert and Will agreed to sail it over to the island. It's moored out there right now, and I thought you might want to take a ride." Simon had a hundred-watt smile, and it was pointed at me far too early in the morning.

"How many boats does this make now, Simon?" I teased. "Of course I'd like to take a ride," I said, planting my feet on the floor and stretching my legs, still sore from yesterday's adventure. "I'm sure you want to go right now?" I asked an obvious question.

"You are correct. I'll go easy on you. How 'bout I meet you down at the pier. I'll take a shore boat over to the mooring, there're some things I want to check out, and you can meet us there in, say…an hour?"

"That sounds great," I said, walking Simon to my door.

"Oh, one more thing, I asked Alice to pack us some lunch. Will you bring it when you come down?" I nodded as Simon closed the door.

After yesterday this was exactly what I needed. I needed to have fun; I could be great fun, I thought as I looked at myself in the mirror. I took a quick tub and lathered my alabaster skin with tanning lotion. I loved tanning lotion; it always made me feel exotic, even though there's not one thing ethnic about me. Maybe it was the smell? Whatever it was, I loved it and I was glowing. I'd bought a new swimsuit that would be perfect for today. I found it in a cute shop in town. Trying it on, I realized it was cut a little lower than I was used to, but I didn't care. It was tasteful and I looked pretty, silky. The white of the swimsuit almost gave me some color. I slipped my loose cotton dress over the suit. Glancing in the mirror one last time, I saw that I was the picture of casual and dare I say…*No more serious Gwen, not for today.* This would be a great day. Simon, the guys, and me. Pulling my hair loosely off my face, I was ready. I threw some things into a canvas bag and headed down the stairs to grab the lunch from Alice.

Simon helped me on the boat and introduced me to Robert and Will. Will was gangly, with a Cartier Baignoire watch and a nice white pair of Oxford bags. His bright red hair and freckled skin made me look tan. He was funny and seemed a very good friend to Simon. Robert was quieter and good looking. He was tall, had golden blond hair, and blue eyes. He looked like a catalog model, but he enjoyed talking with me about everything. He was fascinated with the bird park, asked about the number of species and what it was like working with all those men. He was maybe a little infatuated with me.

We sailed from late morning into early afternoon and moored around the side of the island at Lover's Cove. Robert carried me to shore, which was uncomfortable, but he was the tallest, so Simon insisted. Robert fit perfectly on Catalina Island—he might fit perfectly anywhere, for that matter, with his pants rolled up, darkened by water, and his shirt billowing in the wind. Simon and Will laid out a blanket and we opened the lunch.

"Gwen, will you be on the island all summer?" Robert asked.

"Yes, we should be finished with the bird park in a couple of weeks, but I'll stay until the end of summer. Now that you've done Simon's delivery, how long will you both be here?"

"We need to get back by Wednesday or Thursday for skeet shooting, but we might as well hang out until then. Will?"

"Yeah...sure. It's summer, where else do we need to be?"

I lay out in my new suit on the beach while they all ran around exploring the cove. The warmth felt so good and it was great to relax.

Simon's friends were the epitome of the idle rich. Not to say that my family didn't have money, but these guys were wallowing around in their parents' wealth with no particular place to go and certainly no responsibilities. In spite of that, they were really fun and told great stories about Simon at school. We all enjoyed lunch—and the two bottles of Father's private wine stash Alice had thrown in—and as the sun began to set Simon did really bad movie star impressions that brought us all close to tears of laughter. It was a fantastic day and my mind was fuzzy from the wine. It was time to head back. Robert lifted me to take me back to the boat. This time he smelled even better, a mixture of wine, sweat, and soap. He lifted me as if I weighed nothing, and in my current state it felt perfectly normal to lay my head on his shoulder as he carried me into the water. We sailed back to Avalon right as the sun melted into the horizon. It was a fun day and I was so relaxed. Will and Simon were talking about hitting the town; Robert accompanied me off the shore boat and onto the dock.

"It was great getting to know you, Gwen."

"Likewise," I said.

"Maybe we could get together tomorrow and, I don't know, rent bikes or something?"

"I'd like that, Robert."

"How about we meet for breakfast and then take off around the island. You can show me around."

"That'd be fun. I'll meet you at Joe's around nine?" I asked.

"I'd love that. Until tomorrow." And with that he kissed my hand. Robert was a little dramatic, but I liked him. I turned to see Simon and Will mocking us and kissing each other's hands.

"Nice!" I said, as Robert pushed them both.

"Simon, don't get too crazy tonight. I'll see you at home," I said in my best big-sister voice.

"You got it, sis. No casualties. We're three gentlemen out on the town," Simon sputtered, having had a bit more wine than the rest of us.

"Will, it was a pleasure meeting you and I'm sure I'll see you before you head back." Will smiled.

"Robert, I'll see you tomorrow." Robert was nice and, maybe it was the wine, but I felt certain he had a little crush on me. *Good, I don't think all men are jerks, just you, Michael!*

# CHAPTER SIXTEEN

The next morning Robert and I met for breakfast as planned. Sitting two booths down were Michael and his father. I pretended not to notice, but my heart began to race. I distracted myself by making small talk and of course laughing on cue to make sure Michael knew I was having fun and he was wrong, I wasn't a complete man-hater. *I could be fun, too.* Part of me wondered if he even cared and the other part of me wondered why I cared. *Why was I still reeling from our conversation the other day? Let it go, Gwen.*

Michael rose from his booth as our food was arriving, which was perfect because it gave me something to do as they passed. I pretended not to notice his perfect morning hair or the frame of his chest under his rumpled shirt. One quick glance at Michael, then I made my eyes search the table for salt as he and his father quietly passed. I looked up at Robert after they left and began to understand a little more about chemistry, or the lack thereof.

Robert and I spent the rest of the morning riding bikes around the island. It was enjoyable, but my mind kept returning to seeing Michael again. *What was it about him?* I managed to aggravate myself so much I cut my time with Robert short, complaining of a sore back. He escorted me home and I agreed to meet him at a dance the next evening. He and Will would be leaving the following morning, so I felt I should be there. Robert kissed me on the cheek; it might as well have been Simon. Robert was very attractive and nice, but he wasn't Michael and I needed to figure out why I suddenly wished he were. *What kind of game are you playing, Gwen?* I thought, heading to my room.

Father and I spent most of the next afternoon playing backgammon. I was the master of the game. He, however, made an unforgettable grilled-cheese sandwich for us. Alice nearly killed him for letting the cheese seep into her burners, but he got away with it. After nine matches, Dad took a nap on the couch. I read in my room and wondered what my night at the Saint Catherine would hold.

We could hear the band as we approached the Saint Catherine Hotel later that evening. Simon and I walked through the lobby to the back, where an outside pavilion was lit up and couples were dancing and mingling. Robert and Will were at a small table, dressed in island wear. Robert was even wearing sandals. He looked all too eager to see me.

"Don't you two look lovely," Robert said, hugging me and shaking Simon's hand with a pat on the back.

"Nice sandals—is this island air getting to you?" Simon joked.

Robert laughed. "Must be. We were shopping this morning and the woman in the shoe store told me I had beautiful feet. I couldn't resist. I've never owned a pair, so why not? Right?"

*Wrong,* I thought, still smiling to hide my annoyance. *Are we really talking about Robert's beautiful feet? Does this guy grow more and more shallow every second?*

"Gwen, would you like to dance?" Robert asked as the band began playing "Cheek to Cheek."

I looked at Simon, who could see that Robert wasn't for me, and said, "Sure, Robert, but only one. I promised to dance with my baby brother tonight."

Jumping in right on cue, Simon said, "That's right, Rob, you only get her for one." Robert spun me around the pavilion like a well-schooled dancer—with no connection to me at all. He was on display and was convinced everyone was watching us. *What did I ever see in this man? And why did I waste my favorite blouse for this?* The song was winding down, but Robert did not position himself close to me as we swayed to the final beats of the music. I smiled and thanked him for the dance.

The next song was a Charleston. I turned to leave the dance floor, and there he was. *Mercy! Was this island small enough?* Michael and some pinup in a green dress were on the dance floor and in full swing. I spun Robert around and went back out on the dance floor. This was now a game and my logical mind was spinning, trying to justify my ridiculous behavior. *Michael had been rude and I wanted to prove a point? No, that wasn't it at all,* I thought as Robert led me around in prefect step. *No, I wanted to be the girl in the green dress. I wanted those arms around my waist and those eyes looking at me.* Everything about Michael that enraged me just drew me closer. He challenged me, made me defend my opinions. That's why we fought. He treated me like an equal but stared at me like a woman. Looking at Robert, a perfectly decent man, albeit shallow—and, it turned out, prone to perspire on the dance floor—it hit me. I didn't despise Michael. I wanted him. In that instant I was scared out of my mind.

We joined Simon and Will at the table and ordered another round of drinks. Simon stood to shake someone's hand. The song was over and I looked up and saw Michael. I fumbled through my bag as I heard him introduce his date, Lilly, to everyone at the table. *Collect yourself, Gwen.*

"Lilly, this is Simon's sister, Gwen," he said, smiling at me as if he had a secret no one else knew.

"It's a pleasure to meet you, Lilly. Michael, good to see you. The two of you are lovely dancers," I said, standing, waiting to break for the powder room. I couldn't breathe but I managed to hold it together.

"You and—I'm sorry, what was your name again?" Michael asked, looking at Robert.

"It's Robert, er, Rob. You can call me Rob."

"Yes, my apologies." Michael looked at me. "You and Rob here make a lovely couple, too." His sarcastic simper lingered as I made my escape.

"If you'll excuse me, I need to go to the powder room."

"Hurry back," Simon said, glancing over his shoulder as I fled inside the hotel.

Once inside the doors, I put my hand to my chest. My heart was pounding. I felt exposed, as if Michael knew how I felt about him just by looking at me. I'd lost my edge; I had to get it together. Attraction or no attraction, I valued my wit and I wouldn't be turned to a puddle at the sight of him, although that shirt was the perfect color for him. *Stop it, Gwen.* I applied more lipstick in the mirror, pinched my cheeks, took a deep breath, and back to the table I went, standing tall. I approached the table to see Michael and Green Dress—*What was her name again?*—sitting at our table, hooting it up with Simon and his friends. Robert rose to pull out a chair for me. As I sat, my bare leg brushed Michael's arm. He looked at me and I swear it was his heart that skipped this time. For one moment he looked nervous, and then it passed.

"So, Rob, how long have you known Gwen?" Michael asked.

"Well, we only met the other day, but we're having a great time. I'm sorry I have to leave tomorrow." Robert looked at me, sweetly touching my hand.

Michael smiled. "She looks pretty sorry about it, too."

"We've had a terrific time and I'm sure we'll see more of each other," I said, teasing Michael right back. At this point Robert had no idea what was going on, but Simon did.

"Gwen? Sis? Would you like to dance?" he asked, already pulling my hand. As we began gliding through a waltz, Simon let loose. "What are you doing?"

"What do you mean?" I said, staring at his polished shoes.

"Michael! Gwen, I thought I talked to you about him. What's going on?"

"Nothing. Oh, you think that I…that we're…Oh no, Simon, believe me, there's nothing going on."

"Thou dost protest too much, sweet sister. We need a fire hose to put out those flames."

"What? He has no interest in me."

"So you do like him? Well, believe me, he's interested in you. He hasn't taken his eyes off you since he walked in. It's so obvious. Why are the two of you still fighting like children?"

I didn't know what to say. I felt silly and foolish. For my little brother to say we were fighting like children was an all-time low. The song ended, and as we walked back to the table, Michael stood. I closed my eyes as I moved past him and grabbed my purse. The entire night sky was above, but there wasn't one breath of air for me. He'd gotten to me and I was now embarrassed in front of my brother, who knew me too well.

"Robert, Will, it was a pleasure meeting both of you and spending the weekend together. I'm not feeling well, so I'll be leaving you all to finish out the evening."

Simon stood, "Sis, don't—"

"I really need to be going. Lilly, it was a pleasure. Fabulous dress, by the way. Michael, always a treat. Enjoy the rest of your evening." Lilly smiled and Michael stood there like a statue as I walked out.

# CHAPTER SEVENTEEN

I arrived at the bird park early Sunday morning. I had the day off, but I needed to drop some paperwork by for Charlie before Monday. There were quite a few men there for a Sunday. After some talk about needing to reseed an area of grass in the park that had died, Charlie thanked me for the extra trip, and I turned to head back home. Michael approached, looking as if he were going to walk right through me. I prepared myself for a snide comment about my date, or showing a bit too much leg for such an educated girl. I'd left so abruptly last night, I knew there'd be some comment. I decided to beat him to the punch, so I started to speak, to tell him he, too, was walking a little crooked this morning, or that he…

His finger landed gently across my lips.

I couldn't breathe. His hands fanned out through the back of my hair, cradling my face. His hands were rough, but his touch was sweet. Now I couldn't move. I stared into his eyes, trying to look comfortable and failing miserably. *Where was this coming from? Where was the fight? I was used to the fight.*

I could feel his breath and the quick pace of his heart under my hands that, somehow, were resting on his chest. His lips brushed mine and he pulled back slightly to look at my face. I desperately wanted him to see a sensual, sophisticated woman of the world, but

I feared he only saw me. From the way he was looking at me, that seemed to be exactly what he wanted. I was exactly what he wanted. I closed my eyes and tried to breathe. My head swirled as he pulled my face close to his again. This time our lips met fully, and he kissed me. My body was pressed against him. We'd never been this close; the whole world went fuzzy. I could've been anywhere, anyone could've been watching. I didn't care. He gently pulled away, his hands still cradling my face. I could feel him looking at me as I lingered in this moment, my eyes still closed. Michael's face was still close to me and I could feel his sweet breath as I slowly opened my eyes.

"I'm—I'm sorry if I startled you, but I didn't want to play around anymore. I decided last night to put it out on the table and..." he said still holding my face, as if he was afraid to move.

"And that you did," I said in a gravelly voice. I was still in a daze, but surprisingly calm. I wasn't nervous. I felt suspended and desired. Desired for who I was; I'd not pretended with Michael. He kissed me with such warmth and passion.

"Gwen, I care about you and, and I'm not good at this. I've never felt like this, so I'm pretty sure I'll screw it up, but I had to try," he explained, in a gentle and real voice I'd only heard once before, when we were alone in the interior of the island. He slowly moved his hands down my neck, awaking every sense in my body. Still looking deep into my eyes, Michael moved his hands down my back. Neither of us had looked away for even a moment.

"I care about you, too," I said, feeling slightly sappy, but relishing the time to finally tell Michael how he made me feel. *Well, maybe not exactly how he makes me feel, but it was something.* "If anyone is going to mess this up, I'm sure it will be me, but we have chemistry on our side, right?" We both laughed and I knew then this wasn't a dream. He was the same Michael and I was the same Gwen, but the big secret was out. We kissed and nothing changed.

I felt great, but fear crept back in at the same time. This was all new and what if...*Stop thinking, Gwen*!

"So, how many people do you think are staring at us right now," he said with a smile that lit up the entire overcast morning.

"I'm afraid to look," I said, burying my head in his chest. Michael pulled his arm around my side and we both turned with our heads down to walk toward the golf course, neither of us looking at what we were certain was our audience. Clapping and a few hoots trailed as we quickly escaped. Charlie even bellowed, "Well, it's about time!"

We laughed as we walked along the golf course and up toward the stables. Michael gently kissed me again before pulling his arm off my shoulder and walking beside me. I felt warm and comfortable, but I truly had no idea what I was doing. I was so scared all this time that if I allowed myself to care about Michael I'd lose myself—or worse, once he knew he had me he'd take over and smother me. There was a force when we were together that was powerful.

We walked side by side and talked for hours that day. Not about romance, but about our families, the casino. I told myself we were off to a great start, but my mind was telling me there was no way this would last. He was too good to be true. Great conversation, tremendous respect for my interests and my career, well read, artistic, and beyond beautiful physically. *There was another shoe somewhere and it would drop eventually.*

Over the next few weeks Michael and I worked side by side at the bird park and looked forward to the coming weeks, when it would be filled with its beautiful inhabitants imported from all over the world. The Wrigleys had gone to great lengths and the park would be full of over six hundred species of birds at its completion. I was proud to be a part of the park and I was proud that, given only a menial start, I was able to turn this internship into something worthwhile. Most of all, I was learning so much about people, and the men I worked with in particular. They were great and when you demanded respect and gave it in return they valued you. These men were now my friends and I'd learned there were many shades of gray. *Truly, not all men and women were the same.*

Michael and I were still Michael and I, but without the tension and frustration. We cared about each other and had such a good time together. Michael spent some time sailing with Simon and even went fishing with my father. Mother, of course, wasn't crazy about him, which told me he must be a keeper. We shared picnic lunches together, swam in the ocean, and spent long summer nights talking and walking through Avalon. I taught Michael to enjoy ice cream and he taught me how to drive my father's old beater truck. It all felt so natural, as if we were made for each other. I felt safe and comfortable. Real.

The Wrigleys put on a fund-raiser dinner and special hands-on exhibits for the children at the bird park site one evening. It wasn't finished yet, but they set up white tents and catered a gorgeous event that led into dinner. All of the funds raised were being donated to the University of California's biology program. I volunteered to give tours and work with the children, something I'd never done before. I felt amazing that evening and so full of life and accomplishment. Michael walked me home.

"Have dinner with me tomorrow night?"

"Well, I haven't spent much time with my sister and..." I smiled. "What time?"

"Meet me at Descanso Beach around seven."

"All right, but I think that restaurant only serves lunch."

"Gwen, let me take care of it. Please."

"Descanso at seven it is." I smiled.

We approached my house as the sun was setting. Michael pulled me close and kissed me, but this felt different, more intimate, stronger. My knees buckled and I hung in his arms as he kissed my neck gently and set me back up on my feet. I said good night and turned toward the house. I was floating as I closed the door behind me.

The next day was girls' day out. Simon and Father were off fishing and Alice agreed to take little Stephen for the day. Mary, Mother, and I were off to shop, lunch, and visit the aquarium. Being out with my mother and Mary sometimes felt like an ambush, but I was keeping an open mind. I was in such a good mood, I was certain even my mother could not bring me down. She might try, but I felt strong. The three of us met in the dining room for breakfast.

Alice was in the kitchen feeding the baby and Mary seemed rejuvenated, with her feet up and a beautiful summer skirt set. She seemed rested and sipped her coffee, talking to Mother about Rosaline Platt, Mrs. Platt's youngest daughter, who'd married a Spaniard she met while studying abroad. Gossip was par for the course when Mary and my mother got together, so I sat and listened as Mary went on to say she heard Rosaline had gotten pregnant prior to the wedding day. My mother looked over her glasses in disbelief, probably hoping it was true. Anything to tarnish the halo of Mrs. Platt was always welcome as far as my mother was concerned.

"Where did you hear such a thing?" Mother pretended to defend Rosaline's reputation.

"Agnes, from back home, heard from her husband, who apparently does business with Rosaline's new father-in-law."

"I can't believe it. Well, it goes to show…" She never finished her sentence, took a sip of coffee, tucked the juicy gossip away, and changed the subject. My mother could see I was disgusted and she attempted to save face.

"Gwen, have you seen the aquarium yet?"

"I have not, Mother," I replied curtly.

"I've heard there's an octopus they brought in last week," Alice added.

"Really. Very exciting. Are we ready to go?" I said.

"Mary?" Mother asked.

"Ready. Alice, are you sure you're all right with the baby?"

"It's a joy, Mrs. Jacobsen. You go on and have a great day." Alice smiled.

"Thank you." Mary kissed Alice on both cheeks. Mary really was a kind and warm person. I loved her—couldn't relate to her at all, but loved her deeply.

We went into town and surprisingly had a great day. My mother and Mary were a different breed, but showed glimpses of being the same species as I. We all loved Catalina, for different reasons, but it did bind us. *We all loved shoes and ice cream; relationships could be sustained on this,* I told myself. As long as we stayed away from politics, religion, and the almighty social scene, we were fine. I loved them both.

After the aquarium we walked home and I began wondering what Michael had planned for us that evening.

# CHAPTER EIGHTEEN

After reading in my room and getting ready, it came time to meet Michael at Descanso. I passed my father downstairs as I went to leave.

"Hot date?" he asked.

"A date, Dad. Just a date."

"Michael's a great guy. Have fun." My father gave me a squeeze and I was off.

Walking down the promenade toward Descanso Beach and my date, I was a tornado of thoughts and my heart pounded with anticipation. It was almost as if I were standing outside myself. *Who was this woman*, I thought, *flustered by a touch, consumed by a kiss?* I struggled with how I could feel this way and still be the me I'd worked so hard on. *Was this a fling? Could I return to my normal world, or did I love this man? Even more complicated, did he love me?* I continued to walk, looking out to sea and cherishing the occasional breeze that would dry the summer moisture on my neck.

Approaching Descanso, I saw an incandescent glow. As I drew closer, I began to take in hundreds of candles lining the walkway onto the patio at the beach. Every shape and size of candle was covered in a glass hurricane to protect its flame from the breeze. They continued all the way up the path and along the entire perimeter of the patio. In the center of the large scene, looking out to

"You cook, too?" I said, feeling slightly inadequate and knowing for sure I didn't know another man on the planet who cooked.

"Well, the chefs from the kitchen helped a little, but most of it's my creation," he explained, pouring me some champagne.

"Is that champagne?"

"One of the guys had it smuggled in for me. So, enjoy the music and I'll be right back with the food," he said, throwing a white towel over his arm and bowing to me like a waiter. I laughed and he smiled over his shoulder on his way back to the restaurant.

I sat sipping the champagne, thinking about how out of control this all felt and how magnificent it felt at the same time. Michael returned with the first course and then the second course and finally a decadent chocolate desert he confessed was made by the pastry chef. We spent the whole night talking and laughing until our sides hurt. Michael asked me to dance and we glided along the patio to the soft jazz coming from the gazebo. He held me close. I never wanted the evening to end.

Michael paid the trio as they packed up. The restaurant staff cleared the dishes. I stood with my back to him, shivering a bit from the night air. Footsteps approached me from behind; the warmth of Michael's jacket fell onto my shoulders, followed by his strong arms around me. We stood together, looking out at the endless ocean touched by moonlight.

"Gwen," Michael whispered into my neck. I knew what he was going to say; I could feel it. *Oh, heavens, are you sure? I'm not ready for this.*

"Gwen," he said again, "I—I have such a great time with you."

"Me too," I said, afraid to move.

"I—I've never met a woman like you and I'm sure I never will again. Gwen, I love you," he said as he turned me toward him. Then he said it again, "I love you." He kissed me and my knees went weak, my entire body was limp in his arms. My face felt flushed from the ocean breeze and the champagne, but I'd heard him correctly. *There it was, he loved me, and Lord knows I loved him. I'd never been in love, but this must be it.* My head was swimming from his kisses. I pulled away.

"Michael, I have so much that I want to do." *Perfect Gwen, very romantic.* I couldn't stop myself. "I really want, need, to have my own life. You're wonderful and I've never met a man like you, but I…" I was fumbling and he was looking at me like it didn't matter what I said—he was in love with me. He was beaming and I must have been beaming, too. I couldn't find my words. I wanted to say so much to him and explain that I didn't want to be in a relationship and I needed my independence and I really…and then I said it. Holding his face with both of my hands and looking deep into his eyes I said, "I really care about you, Michael, and this night was so special." I searched his face and he smiled at me. I'm sure he wanted to hear that I loved him, too, and I did, but I couldn't say it. I needed more time.

"Let me walk you home?"

"Michael, I—"

"Gwen, I love you and I know you. When you're ready and you've thought of every possible thing that could go wrong or right, you will realize that you love me, too. I know you do. I can see it in your eyes. I don't need to hear it right now. I feel it."

I smiled and felt like the biggest heel on the planet. *I loved this man, why was it so hard for me to give myself over to that?* Michael walked me home and, holding my face, kissed me and said it again, "I love you, Gwen." Those words hummed in my head as I closed the front door behind me.

I ran upstairs and closed the door. I had a problem. I'd never planned on this. I paced the floor, racking my brain for answers, logical answers. There had to be a way out of this. Then it occurred to me—this had nothing to do with my brain. I needed him. In the pit of my being I was drawn to him. I wanted him more than I wanted to find a way to stay away from him. There was nothing I could do, or wanted to do. I looked out my window and saw his beautiful body walking away. He stopped, turned, and looked up at my open window.

"Good night," I whispered, "I love you, too." I closed the shutters.

# CHAPTER NINETEEN

By the end of the week, everyone at the bird park was on edge and exhausted. Michael and I sat on the patio by the golf course after work. We talked about the week, drank iced tea, and Michael read me poetry. He was becoming part of my life, my routine, and while every now and then my annoying inner voice would chime in with "You need to pay attention where you're going, Gwen, don't get distracted," I didn't care. There was no place I'd rather be when I was with him and no one else I wanted to be with more when we were apart. I closed my eyes, listening to Michael's rich voice as the sun began to drop behind us. He stopped reading.

"Am I putting you to sleep?" he asked, looking up from his book with one eye squinting at me. *Handsome, incredibly handsome.*

"Not at all, I'm simply consumed by your words." I smiled and he laughed, closing the book.

"You know, I'm not sure I've ever read poetry to a woman."

"Really?" I said, opening my eyes.

"I don't think I have."

"You are a captivating reader. I'm surprised."

"Must be too intimate. Poetry and its reader are stripped down…vulnerable," Michael said, pondering his statement.

"Really?" I said with a grin that surprised even me.

"Gwendolyn Ross, where is your mind?" he asked, looking back at me with his warm smile that lit my insides. I blushed as I stood up.

"Well, while you contemplate your thoughts, I'm going to turn the golf course lights on. I promised Charlie I'd take care of it before we left."

"I can..." Michael started to say, until I put my hand up, letting him know I could handle it.

Walking back from turning on the lights, seeing Michael in the distance, I imagined myself gracefully moving toward him. I imagined myself like the woman I saw on the boat coming over to the island. Sensual, alluring, graceful. And then I slipped. Flailing through the air, I fell straight back onto my elbows. Not quite the romantic vision I wanted Michael to see in the moonlight—and it hurt. *Typical Gwen!* I lay there looking up at the darkened sky, trying to figure out how to turn this into either a graceful recovery or a comedy routine, when all of a sudden I felt the spray of water. It wasn't falling down on me like rain, but rather coming up from the ground and arching over me like a water rainbow. The sprinklers had turned on.

By this time Michael was over me, extending his hand to help and trying to contain his laughter. I took his hand and stood, carefully this time. Logic would say at this point we would run to get out of the sprinklers, but we didn't. We stood there, silent, staring at each other, soaking, and bathed in moonlight. Michael's eyes were serious and searching. He touched my face and pulled me to his mouth. It could not have been more romantic if it were a movie. We were suspended under the spray of water in a kiss that was so passionate and yet so sweet and caring that my heart just soared. Michael pulled back and looked at me. Water dripped from his gorgeous, flushed face. We said nothing. The moonlight shone in his eyes and I felt beautiful in the reflection. Cherished. Right then and there something changed. I knew that my heart was gone, it belonged to him. I didn't want to run, I didn't want to make sense of it all. I wanted what was right here in the moonlight. I could have looked at myself through his eyes forever.

The sprinklers stopped, bringing us back down to earth. Michael smiled a wicked smile and, in one swoop, gathered me in his arms.

"Maybe if I carry you we'll actually make it back to the patio." I laughed and threw my arms around his neck.

"I planned this whole thing. See, you think I fell, but it was just a ploy to test your chivalric abilities."

"Really? How am I doing?"

"Beautifully, Mr. Cathner. Really quite beautifully." I smiled at him and rested my head on his shoulder.

We did make it to the patio. Michael set me down and grabbed a stack of beach towels. He wrapped one around my shoulders and took another to dry his hair.

"You're shivering," he said, pulling me close.

"I don't think it's the water," I said, tangled in his eyes.

"Gwen, I…" He pulled the towel up closer to my neck and kissed me again. My head rolled back, exposing my neck. I'm not sure what I was doing; I think I was wrapped up in the romantic movie scene. My clothes were clinging to my body and Michael looked great wet. *Of course he did. Did all men look this good wet? Please, Gwen, could you be any more childish?* Michael moved to touch his lips to my neck. I could feel his warm breath, but he stopped.

"You need to get out of these wet clothes," he said, searching my eyes to see if I was uncomfortable. I was far from uncomfortable. I was the sensual leading lady. I was the romantic lead about to be whisked off to the bedroom by Rudolph Valentino. I slipped again on the wet tile and tried to gracefully fall onto a lounge chair. Michael tried not to laugh, but instantly I was not the buxom siren, I was cute, awkward Gwen, and realistically I'd have no idea what to even do with Valentino. Michael covered me with another beach towel; he pulled a fire drum the workers used in the mornings onto the patio. He lit the drum and flames burst up from the edges. Michael took off his wet leather jacket and turned to me. I could see the outline of his chest through his wet shirt. There they were again, the physical feelings that threatened to override my logical mind. I felt so odd, trapped somewhere between this woman I saw in his eyes and the gawky girl who thought way too much. What did he want from me? Even worse, what was I willing to give him? Standing at my feet and looking into my eyes, Michael began to move his hands under my towel, but again he stopped, ran his fingers through his wet hair, and turned toward the fire. I was going to explode. This was torturous. We were suddenly like two strangers. Michael and I were so good at exchanging witty banter, but suddenly we found ourselves in new territory. I wasn't sure what to call it. I knew I'd never felt it before. My entire body, all of my senses were awake, and I just wanted to be near him. Michael looked like he was having some private conversation with himself.

"You should get out of your stockings," he finally said, quickly glancing back at me and then returning his gaze to the fire. "You'll never get dry with those things on."

I said nothing and began taking my stockings off. The towels covered my legs and Michael was looking in the opposite direction, but it felt intimate. We said nothing, which was making me really uncomfortable. I liked words, I was good at conversation, but this was painful.

"Wet stockings removed, as instructed," I joked, trying to lighten the mood.

Michael smiled, but turned back toward the fire as if he could not look at me. What had changed? Why was this all of a sudden so awkward? I swiveled my bare feet around to touch the cold tile. I stood, weak-kneed, and walked behind him. The siren returned. I wrapped my arms around his chest. It was bold, but I wanted to break through whatever this was that all of a sudden felt so strange. Michael's skin was warm and firm. I took a towel and dried his chest through his wet shirt. I'm not sure how much good I was doing, but there was no way I was taking that shirt off. I felt certain I would pass out.

Michael stopped my hands and turned to me. It was as if he was asking me a question. He reached out and touched my face. I sat back down on the lounge and he sat next to me, staring at me, still touching my face as if he was seeing me for the first time. Wet hair must look good on me because he gently, still trembling from the cold, kissed my lips. Just my lips, softly, nothing more. I touched him and I could feel his heart pounding. My hands ran over his chest—they clearly had a mind of their own. His body was beautiful. I'd spent so much time in his eyes, but tonight I took in the whole of him and it was overwhelming, but it all felt so right. I was making myself dizzy. I lay back on the lounge and looked up at the stars. My mind was swimming and I tried to control my breathing. Everything felt new and I wanted these feelings. I was ready to explore this side of myself; at least I thought I was. Michael carefully suspended himself above me and my mind kicked right back in. His look was different and I'm sure mine was, too. Things were growing, we were closer, and while I wasn't scared, I was nervous. Michael looked down at me and kissed me. I'd never wanted a man more in my life. I wasn't sure what I would do with him, but I knew I didn't want him to leave. I felt alive and at that moment, I would have run off with Michael anywhere. Not the smartest feeling, but there it was. Michael pulled himself up and sat at the end of the lounge, putting my legs over his lap. I could hear him take in a deep breath and he patted my legs.

"I should get you home, Gwen."

"What?"

He smiled, amused by my response. "We need to get home."

Still dazed, I sat up. "I don't want to go home."

"Yes…"

I kissed him, hoping he would change his mind.

"Yes, you do," he said.

"You—we have to work in the morning and"—he smiled again—"I need to get you home."

I swung my legs around and sat next to him. Leaning over, I buried my head in his chest. Michael wrapped his arm around me and held me. We sat quietly for a moment and listened to each other's breath. I was beginning to come back to my senses. So much of me didn't want to wake up from this, and then there was the part of me that wondered why Michael stopped. *Did he stop with other women? I felt certain he didn't, so why not kiss me and touch me? I wasn't looking for anything scandalous, but we were right there, under the moonlight. Shouldn't I be the one to say, "Oh no, Michael. I can't!" Shouldn't I be the one batting my eyelashes and asking him to control his passion for me? What was this? Did he not feel passion for me?* He was now standing and putting his jacket back on. Not a word.

"Michael? Is something wrong?"

He stared at the fire. "Not at all, I—"

"You what?" I stood, slipping into my soggy shoes and feeling a little self-conscious.

Michael turned to me and straightened my blouse. He then pushed a wet piece of hair out of my face. I felt foolish. Maybe he didn't see me this way. *Maybe he loved me like you love a piece of art, or your favorite sister. Oh, please don't let this turn out to be, "Gwen, you're a sweet girl…" Please let him see me as a woman.* He could tell

I was confused and gently kissed me. I closed my eyes and kissed him back, softly.

"I love you," he said, sounding a little choked up. I kept my eyes closed. His warm breath caressed my ear. "And I want to—I want to be with you. Dash it all, I need you, but you're too..." His lips rested on my neck.

"Too what?" I pulled away.

He looked into my eyes. "Too important, too much. As much as I want you—and, Gwen, believe me, every part of me wants you—you wouldn't be a fling. Once I've got you under my skin, I'll never want anyone else again."

I put my hand to his cheek. "Is that a bad thing?"

"No, but it's a dangerous thing. I won't be able to come back from this if—"

"If what?"

"When you, I don't know. I think I need to get you home," he said, grabbing a handful of sand to put out the fire. Michael wrapped his arm around me as we walked toward the house. I rested my head on his shoulder and I replayed his words in my head. He was nervous and scared of his feelings for me. *That made two of us.* I was different. He must've always kept a safe distance with other women, but this was more. Not simply physical, he wanted all of me, and as much as I was willing to kiss and hold him forever, I'd not told him what was in my heart. I didn't know how to tell him and give in to what my heart wanted without giving him everything. *Why was everything so complicated?*

Michael walked me home as he always did, and stopped at the driveway. We were both exhausted. Even though we'd not done anything more than kiss, I could not stop smiling as we stared at each other, hands intertwined. Breaking the silence, Michael said, "I know we both have to work tomorrow, but let me take you dancing tomorrow night?"

"I'd love to…I would, but I can't. I have dinner with my family tomorrow night. You're on your own tomorrow." I smiled. "See, you should've never brought me home."

"Ah, really? Well, I suppose I can be without you for one night," he said, flashing the smile. "Have a good time," he conceded, and kissed me softly. I opened the door and he moaned, letting me slip into the house. As our fingers parted I closed the door behind me. I quietly tiptoed up the stairs into my room. When I was behind my door I let out a sigh of pure elation and confusion. We would figure this out…I'd figure this out. *I could give part of myself to Michael and still keep part of myself for me…right?* I was delirious and exhausted. I realized I only had a few hours to sleep before I'd be expected at the bird park. My face touched the cool sheets. *In my dreams…I'll work this out in my dreams,* I thought as I drifted off to sleep.

Alice knocked on my door what seemed like five minutes later.

"Miss Gwen. It's morning…are you going to have breakfast before you leave?" Knocking again she said, "Miss Gwen…it is almost nine o'clock…don't you need—"

*Nine o'clock?* I sat straight up. "Yes, Alice. I'll be down in ten minutes. Please pack me a breakfast to take with me. I'll need to leave right away."

"Sure, ma'am. I'll have it ready when you come down. Good morning, Miss Gwen."

"Good morning, Alice," I said, cracking the door. "Thank you for waking me." I smiled as I closed the door again.

I was so tired, but I didn't care. I looked at myself in the mirror. My hair was all over the place and my lips were still pink from last night. My skin was flush and glowing, partly from my lack of sleep, but mostly from the feeling pulsing through my entire body. I quickly dressed and headed down to grab my bag.

"Oh, Gwen? Before you run off…What color was the sunrise this morning…you know, when you got home?" Simon asked, giggling out loud as I ran past the dining room.

I stopped, smiled back at him and replied, "It was a warm orange with small flecks of red and…a hint of purple." I twirled toward Alice, kissed her on the cheek, took my breakfast, and I was out the door into the crisp, moist air of the morning. I hadn't even seen my parents' faces as I whirled out the door. *Glad I could provide amusement, Simon*, I thought. I smiled all the way to work.

# CHAPTER TWENTY

I was fifteen minutes late and, looking back, I should've stayed in bed. The hustle and bustle was just getting started as I approached the site, but something was wrong. Charlie was standing by a truck with several boxes. He was looking into one and shaking his head. I dropped my bag by the entrance, next to several lunch boxes and hard hats. I was already embarrassed to be late and I sprinted over to Charlie.

"Good morning," I said. That was a mistake.

"Really? Is it a good morning for you, Miss Ross?"

"Is something wrong?"

"You could say that. You see what I have here is a truckload of heating lamps. They're a custom order. Researched and purchased by my bright and articulate intern. She's gone out of her way to prove to me that she's the man…pardon me, the wo-man for the job." He took a breath; I was filled with panic. This could only end badly. "Custom order, did I say that?" I nodded. "You know what's so important about a custom order? It can't be returned." My heart sank as my mind spun with a million questions. *What's he talking about? Why would they need to be returned? I ordered them myself. Please, get on with it! What's wrong?*

"Why would they need to be returned? Because my bright intern ordered the wrong lamps. A week of research and travel to the mainland and they're wrong! Gwen, these are not what we discussed. These are a different model all together. What the hell were you thinking? Where was your head?"

By this time everyone, and I mean everyone, was staring at me. Here I was again, an entire site full of men and I was the odd "wo-man" out. I still could not get my head around it. *I checked and double-checked that order, how could it be wrong*? I thought as I stared at Charlie and allowed him to finish his demeaning tirade. My face felt bright red and my head was pulsing.

Taking a deep breath, I asked the driver, "Could I please see the paperwork for the order?"

The paperwork showed row after row of the wrong equipment. This wasn't what I ordered and this was not what Charlie and I discussed. I looked up at the address. It was our address. I ran back to my bag and pulled out my copy of the order I'd phoned in over a month ago. I put the paperwork side by side and flipped through each page, my head about to explode and completely aware of the million eyes staring at me…*What was going on?* And there it was, the tiny little star in the order column that directed me to a short paragraph on the back that read: "Item discontinued, substitute shipped to ensure delivery. If these substitutions will not work for your project please contact us and we will process a refund. We appreciate your business and apologize for the inconvenience."

I don't really know what happened next, except to say I lost my mind. I was happy this morning. While I couldn't say it out loud, I was in love. This internship was wonderful—thanks in part to my hard work and my ability to compromise. I'd grown up working here. I felt good about everything as I raced from the house this morning, but standing there I felt like none of it mattered. I was being punished for relaxing, living a life. Punished with one hysterical slap in the face. *It's an order for heat lamps. Would Charlie have exploded if I weren't a woman? This all felt like a setup. Like everyone was really waiting for me to fail.* I looked up from the paperwork at Michael, who was now standing by the entrance to the aviary. He was frozen, not sure whether to smile. I looked around at this sea of men. The pressure was immense.

"Mr. Chambers, if you'd look..." *Don't cry, Gwen!* "Please, look at the writing at the end of the paperwork." I handed him the invoice. "I ordered the correct items, but they're discontinued. They sent these as substitutes. We'll need to call them for a refund. I—"

"Jesus, why didn't..." He looked at the driver. "Gwen, I...Jesus, I'm sorry. I'm under so much pressure with this thing and this was the last straw." He put his hand on my shoulder and I fought back the urge to completely collapse. The noise of work began to fill the air again. It was as if someone hollered: "Nothing more to see here." They'd all stopped working to watch the train wreck and now that I'd narrowly escaped, everyone was free to return to work. A deep sigh of relief left my lungs.

I kept myself together and said, "Charlie, it was easy to miss. I'll call them right now and take care of it." I turned to the driver, gave him back his paperwork, and said, "I'll call your company right now, but for now we don't have a place to keep equipment that we didn't order and we don't need. Please take this back to the dock and have it sent back."

He hesitated for a moment before I shot him my best "I'm mad. Don't start with me" look. He covered the boxes and was gone. Charlie looked at me and smiled. A simple smile and he was back behind his glasses and drafting plans. I looked at Michael, who was smiling slightly now, and then I slowly walked away from the whole damn thing. I needed to walk away. I walked for quite a while, silent and numb. I found myself at the small new art gallery setting up on the island. Simon was standing at the entrance, talking with a gentleman in an orange vest. He was working with this man and helping him set up his exhibit. Simon was an art aficionado and especially loved giving new artists the benefit of his extra income.

"Simon," I called from across the street.

"Gwen." He smiled, pardoned himself, and ran across to embrace me. I started to cry.

"What? What's wrong?"

"Nothing, I'm so—oh, I'm so angry." I pulled back, gently wiped my tears in embarrassment, and told him what had happened. I wasn't kind and said everything I'd wanted to say to Charlie.

"How dare he, he would have never spoken to me like that if I weren't a—"

"I disagree," Simon interrupted.

We sat down at an outside table and Simon said, "You know, big sister, there are pressures on men, too." He was serious. "What you experienced was a man-size pressure. Charlie wasn't yelling at you because you're a woman, he was yelling at you in spite of you being a woman."

Simon was uncharacteristically serious, mature, and...right. He continued as I sat silently listening to valuable insight. "If he'd looked at you as a woman he would have never blown up like that, you'd be too fragile to handle it. But he yelled at you like any other man he was working with. What you experienced wasn't chauvinism, but the feeling of incredible pressure and responsibility men feel every day. We're constantly worrying, checking our work, and, if you're going to have a career, you need to get used to this," he finished, as if to say *be careful what you ask for.*

"Simon, are you trying to say—"

"Sis, it goes both ways. Men have pressures. I have them, too. Sometimes I think it's worse."

Nothing in college prepared me for what'd happened. *What if I'd made a mistake?* I was sure at some point in my career I'd mess up. I'd have to own up to it and find a way to move forward. For the first time I saw my brother as a man and I felt for him. I didn't envy him or his freedom. It wasn't all green grass on the other side. I kissed Simon and thanked him for listening to his crazy sister.

I'd now seen the downside of a career and I began to understand why women stayed home. It was hard enough to work as a man, but the pressure and the eyes waiting for a mess-up as a woman were all that more intense. This whole thing was an affirmation that I'd really need to be on my toes if I was ever going to have a shot at a career. At that moment Michael's face popped into my head and, for the first time in the last few weeks, that image wasn't a good thing. Taking a deep breath, I returned to the site, picked up the phone, and called our supplier. *Back to work.*

# CHAPTER TWENTY-ONE

I was relieved to have a night at home, especially after the narrowly avoided fiasco that morning. Dinner with my family wasn't normally something I looked forward to, but tonight it would provide a much-needed break from the "to love Michael or not to love Michael" debate. I was starting to annoy myself; everything seemed so difficult once it got into my head. I did not see how I could float around on a cloud, like I'd been with Michael, and still live in the world of Charlie yelling at me this morning. *How can those two coexist?*

I was thankful tonight's conversation would consist of Mary's baby talk, Father inquiring about what Simon was going to do after summer, and my mother's mind-numbing island gossip and squabbles. I read for an hour in my room and then went down to dinner.

The table was perfect, as always. Everything seemed as I predicted, until Mary entered the room with George trailing close behind. She was dressed for dinner, but looking a little disheveled and she clearly wanted nothing to do with George. I thought they might've had a fight. Mother ushered us all to the table.

"Gwen, you look lovely tonight, dear," my mother exclaimed, surprising me beyond words.

I managed a "Thank you, Mother. It must be my new hair clip. You look lovely yourself."

"Must be, you look very feminine and just right."

I laughed. "Well, I did clean the dirt out from under my nails when I got home from the bird park today."

Mother was not amused, but she feigned a laugh with my father.

Mary glared at me.

"All right, let's get this show on the road," Father bellowed, smashing his cigar in an ashtray Alice was holding next to his chair.

Mary glared at me again. I smiled—that was clearly not the right thing to do.

"Oh, please." She rolled her eyes and threw her napkin into her lap. Mary was angry and for the moment it appeared her husband was safe. She was angry, steaming really, at me. "I'm so sick of your holier-than-thou attitude. Little Miss College Graduate. Are you really thinking things will be different for you?" she snarled with a venom I'd not heard before. I said nothing.

"We're the same animal, Gwen. Our life is mapped out for us. The only difference is you'll have more intelligent conversations at your cocktail parties and summer soirées." Running her hands across her face, she said, "George and I were in love once and passionate and I had dreams, too. George looked at me like I was the only woman in the world—before he started looking at every other woman. Before I became the most boring mother and housewife that ever lived." She began to stumble over her words. Mary was exhausted. The baby had been up almost every hour last night and I was obviously the focus of her anger.

"So, missy, don't prance around here with love and hope and I-can-have-it-all, because let me tell you, you can't. You have to choose, Gwen. Life is all about choices and you have to live with the ones you make." Mary finished with a fake sarcastic smile.

"You're just tired, Mary, and I..." I'd finally found my words.

"Damn right! I am tired and it's about time someone in this family cut through the bull you keep dishing out. You must be better than all of us. Lord knows Daddy thinks you are." She spun around to look at my father, who then looked at my mother.

Mary continued, "I'm now the boring married daughter, dark circles under my eyes, the cast-aside. Let me tell you something: Once upon a time I was a shining star. I was the one everyone wanted. I was beautiful."

This was turning really sad now, so I tried, "You're still beautiful, Mary. You're a beautiful woman and an incredible mother." And then things got worse.

"Tell that to this…jerk," she spewed, slapping George on the back.

"Mary, stop. This is not necessary. You need to rest. I think you're beautiful and you're a wonderful wife." George took her hand and, with a flushed face, tried to calm her down.

"I don't want to be a wonderful wife. I want to be sensual, alluring, or an engaging conversationalist. I want to be wanted." Mary tried to get up from the table and George stood to help her. This was a nightmare and I felt for George and for Mary, though I wasn't sure where all of this was coming from.

"Get your hands off me," she snapped.

George looked into Mary's glazed eyes. "Mary, sweetheart, you're making a scene. Please come upstairs with me and we can talk about this privately. You can have your dinner brought upstairs. No one expects you to be…" He smiled at my father, who was on his second glass of scotch. My mother fiddled with her napkin, hoping Mary would somehow disappear. I'd seen that look countless times, directed at me.

"You're such a piece of…George!" Mary said, pounding on his chest as he gently motioned her up the staircase. They were halfway up the stairs when Mary collapsed and George swept her up in his arms and carried her to their room.

No one ever really knew if George had been unfaithful or if Mary was jealous of every other woman in his life. George seemed like a nice guy. Painfully ordinary and quiet, but a good man nonetheless.

Sitting in uncomfortable silence as we continued eating, I thought the issue had to be Mary. She'd had her share of exciting and sometimes dangerous boyfriends. She'd settled in with George and he took good care of her. Someone needed to take care of Mary. She might argue that she could take care of herself, but she was wrong. Mother raised her to be completely dependent and she simply transferred her neediness from my parents to George when they married. She never needed to find herself and that was all right with everyone. We loved Mary the way she was, but obviously Mary was struggling with something inside of her that wanted more, or she was simply trying to figure out how to juggle a new baby. Instead of looking into herself, she blamed George and he took it. He smiled at her with the same affection he did the day they were married. I think she hated him, because no matter what outburst she came up with, he was never fazed. He just cleaned up the mess with a clever, dismissive one-liner and quietly brought her back down. Secretly Mary wanted him to yell, fight back, and show some passion for her. But that wasn't George's way.

"OK…well, that was unfortunate," Mother said, putting her napkin on the table. "Would anyone like some more roast?" I tried to pretend I didn't hear her. *My mother was a trouper—no matter what the obstacle, she just got out the good china and kept going.*

Mary was right to a certain extent; you can't have it all, and I knew that. I wasn't Mary, I kept telling myself. Michael and I were different. I didn't spend my life planning my wedding. I never wanted Michael to happen. That made me, that made *us*, different. Mary walked into this life she now found herself in. She wanted a husband and children and maybe now she was finding they were not enough. *Michael and I are free spirits. We both want our own identities and he loves me the way I am. That'll never change. Besides, we're living for right now and we don't know what tomorrow will hold. We love each other. That doesn't mean we're getting married.* My mind wandered to last night, Michael kissing me. We were in deep, but it was all right.

The annoying voice in my head kept yelling, *Do you want to end up like Mary or, even worse, your mother?* I ignored the voice. I was the same person I was when I arrived on the island. Focused, driven, but now I had someone to share things with, an equal. *There was a happy ending here. Please let there be a happy ending here.*

# CHAPTER TWENTY-TWO

We all adjourned to the living room for dessert. I went upstairs to get into something more comfortable. Mother noticed and ignored as I returned in the lounge pants I was pretty sure she hated. Mother would never be big on progress, or comfort, for that matter.

"Get me outta here!" Simon whispered urgently, handing his empty cake plate to Alice as I stood by the window.

"You mean the dessert didn't help? Why, I'm so surprised," I said, quietly mocking my mother. "Where would you like to go, Mr. Ross?"

"Out there." He pointed toward Avalon.

"Our excuse tonight?" I asked with a smile.

"We—we…need to pick up, we need to go…Ah, hell I don't know, but I need to get out of here."

"How about, we're going for a walk to check on the boat?"

"You're a genius. Let's go."

"I can't go like this…in pants. I look like a man."

"Who cares? We don't have time to change. Time to get while the getting's good," Simon said, taking my arm and pulling me toward the door. He grabbed his coat off the rack and exclaimed, "Gwen and I are going to check on the boat, be back in a few." We were out the door as my mother started to say something. Simon was putting his coat on as we ran from the house. He turned toward me with his hands in his hair and a crazy look on his face.

His expression made me laugh, but my head was still buzzing from the scene back at the house. What had happened that even Mother couldn't squelch with dessert? Mary completely fell apart and we all stood there like spectators. All of us, that is, except for poor George. Maybe he wasn't poor George at all; maybe he was guilty George. My thoughts were swimming as we went down the hill. I couldn't make sense of any of it. I only knew Mary looked miserable. *Was that love?* She seemed so defeated; I knew that was what happened to women, even women who wanted to be taken care of, like Mary. Their whole being was basically stolen. That would never happen to me. Mary was wrong. I loved Michael, but I loved myself more. We were beautiful together, but I'd never let that ruin me. My cheeks were warm in the chill of the night air. Simon gave me his coat and, luckily, my pants were wool.

"That was wild, wasn't it?" Simon exclaimed. "Who thought sis had those big-girl words in her?"

"Simon, it's not funny, she was really upset."

"Oh, I know it's not funny. It's sort of funny. Did you see Mother's face? It thought she was going to—"

"Simon!" I interrupted and stood still. "She was in pain. Our sister was in pain and obviously at her wits' end to completely break down like that. It was sad."

"OK, OK, but Gwen, it's not like Mary was ever the pinnacle of mental health or stability. Remember when she and George were dating and she talked about him all the time and what their wedding would be like and their children and on and on..." Simon said, rolling his hand at the wrist to show a wheel. "She was obsessed and she got everything she thought she wanted. She'll be fine. I bet she's just off balance from having the baby. Mary is right where she belongs. She needs to adjust, that's all."

"Or the last few bits of her individuality were dying off right in front of us," I said seriously, looking at Simon.

"Oh, don't be so dramatic, Gwen. Mary is not you. I'm not sure she ever had any individuality and if she did discover some, I'm sure she chased it off long before George. He loves her and she loves him. They're right for each other and she's just acting crazy. Like I said, they'll be fine."

I wasn't so sure, but I was tired and I gave in with a slight smile to Simon.

"Now, where should we go to wash off this gloom and doom?" Simon asked, looking around at the silent town of Avalon. Everything was closed and the sound of the gentle waves lapping on the beach accompanied the dim moonlight above. There was a faint sound up ahead as we walked toward the Tuna Club. They'd had a tournament today and it seemed like the patrons were still trading stories and exaggerations. As we approached Simon snickered at me.

"What?" I smiled.

"You know what we should do?"

"Sit on the beach and I can watch you finish the rest of this flask?" I said, holding up his shiny little pocket companion.

"That won't last me the night—you should have fun too."

"All right, what do you suggest?"

"Come here," he said, almost in a whisper. As I approached, Simon buttoned up the jacket I was wearing, pushed my hair to the side, and put his driving cap on my head.

"What? What are you doing?"

"This is perfect, you're already wearing those pants and no one will know the difference." He continued to straighten me up.

"Simon, what?" I looked at him and he pointed to the Tuna Club. "Oh no. Are you crazy? I'm not going in there. They'll throw us out on our ear and why would I want—"

"You know you want to come into the inner lair of the man world. Aren't you the slightest bit curious?"

"Curious about what? 'My fish was this big!' 'No, my fish was bigger!' No, I can't say I'm curious," I said, laughing at myself.

"Fine, you're scared. I understand. Such a girl!"

"Is that supposed to work?"

Simon smiled his devilish smile.

"Oh, all right!" I said. "But if we get caught you're the one who will look like the fool. I'll only be the silly woman." Simon started giggling like a schoolboy. As we walked up the white, creaking stairs of the Tuna Club, I held the railing and my breath.

For a moment as we approached the greeter I wondered if I'd taken off my earrings. Panic hit me as the large man said, "Si, where've you been?"

"Jack, good to see you. We heard the party and thought we'd come by." Simon grabbed my shoulder and introduced me as Gerald. I kept my head down as we approached the bar—Jack didn't notice. I peeked up from under Simon's cap; no one seemed to care about me. I'd worried that the minute I walked in some alarm would go off, but nothing. The place was packed. There was faint music playing at the end of the bar, but there was really no need. The laughter and banter coming from five or six groups behind me were enough to create their own choir. I carefully looked around. This was historic, the Tuna Club. To my knowledge no other woman had ever been in this place. It was an exclusive fishing club for men only. Father and Simon were members and so were many other famous and not-so-famous men who vacationed or visited the island. Catalina was becoming famous for its big-game fishing, and men took this very seriously. I'd never been deep-sea fishing myself, but the stories my father tells are nothing short of pirate adventures. Exaggerated, I'm sure, but another example of the unfettered fun of being a man. The Tuna Club was exactly what Simon said, a lair.

The energy was bouncing off the walls as Mac, the bartender, slid over. "What'll it be, Si?"

Simon smiled and said, "Scotch straight up for both of us, sir."

"Comin' up," Mac replied, looking curiously at me but not bothering to ask. I looked around at the pictures behind the bar, lifting my head enough to take in the sights.

"Can you believe this?" Simon whispered with a giggle.

"No. Why'd you order me scotch? I can't drink scotch."

"Sure you can; it's all part of the image," Simon said, striking a match on the bar and lighting a cigar.

"Don't even think about it," I said, referring to the cigar. I love the smell, but would never smoke one. Rumor has it somewhere in our lineage we had a grandmother who smoked a pipe, but there was no way I was going to be the cigar-smoking sister. Simon smiled, turned his back to the bar, and rested both elbows behind him. He was enjoying toying a little with my discomfort. I began to relax as a sip of smooth scotch slid down my throat. *What was the worst thing that could happen?* I thought with a smile, and then it happened.

"You know what we need in here?" some man from behind me bellowed. "Women!"

"We don't want women in here," another slurred. "We want them waiting for us at home." They all erupted in laughter. My face began to feel warm. Simon continued to smoke his cigar and laughed a little for appearances.

"Yeah, but not all of us have a woman at home," the same man continued.

"Oh, sit down, Joe, and stop your bellyachin'," a familiar voice joked. I knew that voice and my entire body froze except for my heart, which was pounding. The men laughed at the last comment, things settled down for a moment, and then...

"Michael doesn't need a woman. He's already got the cream of the crop. Ain't that so?" The man slurred again, "He caught himself a Ross and a mighty pretty one, too." The men continued to laugh as chairs scraped on the floor behind me.

Simon finally turned toward the bar. "Gwen, we should go."

"Joe, sit down," I heard Michael say from behind me.

"Aw, come on, Michael, tell us the story how you reeled that one in. We're all buddies, right?" the man continued to slur and I knew Simon was right. It was time to leave, but I couldn't get out of my seat.

I was frozen there as the laughter subsided and Michael said, "Joe, you're jealous because you were never any good at the catch. The best part is the catch. The art is in the catch. Once you've caught 'em the fun is over." His voice was animated. He'd been drinking, but it was Michael.

"Yeah, but this time I think little Miss Ross has caught you, my friend." Joe howled again as the table of men erupted in oohs and ahhs.

"That'll never happen, boys. The fish will always be the fish and the fisherman is always the fisherman." Michael belted his final victory jab to his excited spectators clinking glasses among the laughter.

*I'm a fish*, I thought. *Gwen, Gwen*, the little voice in my head said, *They're all the same. When are you going to learn?* I didn't want to believe my annoying voice, but after listening to Michael's performance, how could it be wrong? I, Gwendolyn Ross, was reduced to a fish on a line by a man I deeply loved so he could entertain his fellow apes. I couldn't turn around, but Simon was right next to me, perhaps a little worried I'd make a scene. He needn't worry—there was no way I could even stand, let alone make a scene.

Simon hooked his arm around mine and said, "Gwen, get up. We need to leave." I shot down the last of the scotch in my glass and lifted myself off the stool, hanging on Simon. As we walked out of the Tuna Club in the shadows, I glanced back at Michael, who was now seated, leaning back in his chair with his hands behind his head. Pleased with himself and yet a pathetic caricature trapped in a world of machismo and ridiculousness. He loved me and I wasn't a fish to him, but if he couldn't tell these idiots that, then there was nothing left to talk about. *Run*, was all I thought as the cool evening air hit my face, clearing away the stale liquor and cigar cloud. *Run, Gwen, go home and get out of here.*

"Gwen, he was joking. It was harmless. He was drunk," I heard Simon mutter as I handed him his coat and took off running toward the house. *Never again. I'd let myself get distracted and I...* The tears streamed down my cheeks. As I ran up the stairs to my room, for a moment I hoped I'd simply had too much to drink. *This wasn't really as bad as it seemed, everything was heightened because of the alcohol...this would all be fine in the morning*, I tried to convince myself as my head was spinning. I lay down on my bed with a horrible ache that I wasn't sure had anything to do with the scotch.

# CHAPTER TWENTY-THREE

The next morning my eyes opened, greeted by a throbbing headache and a heartache ten times worse. It wasn't a dream, nor a night of silliness. Mary's breakdown, Michael's…whatever that was. It had all happened and it was morning. *I needed to go home. This was not my life. None of it was. I was on the cusp of a great life for myself. I didn't need any of this. I needed to grow up and get on with my life.*

I dressed quickly, asked Alice to pack my things on my way toward the stairs, and ran out the door before my parents, Simon, or Mary were even awake. I was wounded and in survival mode. It was time for flight.

I knocked on Michael's door. He was awake, with coffee in hand.

"I missed you." He smiled, and pulled me close. I wanted to let him wrap me in his arms and forget about this whole mess, but that wouldn't happen. I pulled away from him and quietly said, "I'm leaving. I only have about an hour before I need to get to the boat." I couldn't look at him. "I wanted to say good-bye and thank you for a wonderful time and…" I tried to smile as I moved back out the door. Michael gently took my wrist, pulled me back in, and closed the door behind me.

"Why are you doing this? What happened?"

"This won't work and I can't—"

"You can't what? Love me? You don't want this?" he asked, shaking his head. "You can't what?" He was in pain and there was nothing I could—well, there was nothing I *would* do.

"We belong together, we fit—"

"No, Michael. I'm me, not we. This has been great but it's not reality. We're on this beautiful island and you're…" I took a deep breath. "But this isn't what you build a life on. I've a plan for myself and being Mike's girl isn't part of it. I can't be distracted at this point in my life. I've invested too much—"

"What am I taking away from you? I want you to have whatever makes you happy. Become a doctor, whatever you want."

"Michael, that's so easy to say, but not long from now, you'll want a home and children and I'll wake up Mrs. Michael Benjamin Cathner and—" I turned away because I wanted to tell him that I believed the fairy tale and that he was different and we could have it all, but I knew better.

"What changed? Where's this coming from? If we love each other the rest will work—"

"No, it won't!" I raised my voice. "Love blinds you and makes you do stupid things. Things you regret later. Love is…please stop looking at me like that. I was at the Tuna Club last night with my brother. I heard you with those guys." My heart was racing with equal parts of ache and anger. "You sounded like every other guy. You can't help yourself, you—you didn't say you loved me. I was a fish, a catch. You are—"

"What the hell are you talking about? This is crazy, Gwen. Why were you there? What'd I say?"

"'The art is in the catch,' that's what you said. 'Fish will always be fish and you're the fisherman.'" I looked him squarely in the eye.

"We were drinking and they were goading me about being with you. It was stupid. Did you want me to declare my love to that group of men? Come on, don't do this!"

"I'm leaving. I need to get back to my life and you've got the casino to finish. It was fun." My eyes started to burn as a tear ran down my face and I quickly brushed it away. He knew I was already gone and I could tell he thought I was crazy, but I didn't care. I needed to get away from this before it destroyed me. Slowly, he took my face in his hands and gently pressed his soft lips to mine. As he closed his eyes tears streamed down his face and around our lips. His hands were gently trembling and I pulled away. He looked at me longingly. I swallowed back everything I was feeling and I gave him nothing in return. I couldn't; this was self-preservation.

"You're going to throw all of this away over some stupid comments to a bunch of drunk men? You're running and it has nothing to do with last night." Michael looked at me for a response. Hoping he could pull me back and save me before I'd finished the final brick in my wall. He was too late and he could see it in my eyes. He was hurt and it was over. That night at the golf course he'd told me he could not let me in, that he felt vulnerable, that I'd eventually leave. Here I was proving him right, and his pain turned to anger. Protection, I was sure, for his breaking heart. Even though he'd been a buffoon, I wouldn't talk to him, so he struck back. "All right then, you've got to get going," Michael said softly. I could see the wall rebuilding in his eyes. His face grew cold, and with two quick swipes, his tears were gone.

"Michael," I said, reaching for his arm.

"Don't!" He raised his voice and pulled away from me. "Go home. Don't waste one more minute of your time with me. Goodbye, Gwen."

"I don't want to hurt you. I know what we have is—"

"Oh, please. You haven't hurt me. I'll be perfectly fine. There's another Gwendolyn Ross coming in on the morning boat, right? Isn't that my persona, my image? Leave," he said, stabbing me with a glare I had never seen before in his perfect eyes.

I walked out, expecting to feel some sort of liberation. I'd ended the one thing that threatened my independence, my sense of self. Right? I began to sob. The tears ran down my face and pooled at my neck. Gasping for air, I started to run toward the house, exactly as I'd run last night after hearing Michael at the Tuna Club. I was so angry last night. Where was that anger? This run home was much worse. I'd fixed the problem, but my mind was still racing and my heart...my heart was in pain.

My body gave in to the ache; I stopped at the corner and buckled over onto a bench near the water. Never in my life had I experienced this. The poems in the book Michael gave me spoke of heartache in such eloquent and almost beautiful terms. *Perhaps the ability to see heartache in that light came later, upon reflection?* Right now this pain was ugly and wretched. There were no elaborate words for this. My soul was suffocating.

A couple of days ago I could barely contain myself within my body. I was in love and cherished and liberated. One night changed that? I felt dizzy. *What am I doing? it's too late to turn back now, Gwen.* I had issued my own death sentence. As I took in the full impact of what I'd done, it occurred to me that this was merely the beginning of the pain. As intense as this was right now in this moment, it was just the beginning. There would be many more tears and many more days of emptiness and aching. *Why would anyone bring this kind on pain on herself? Why didn't I say, "I love you desperately, Michael. You were a complete idiot last night and I'll be mad at you for a while, but..."?*

I'd closed the door and left him standing there. He was soaked in disbelief and I left him there. *What kind of a cold person does that over one night of stupidity?* He was right, there was so much more to this. I was desperate to be different and Michael was a different kind of man, but a man nonetheless. He would get older and have needs and roles for me I wasn't willing to play. I set us both up.

I was waiting for him to be less than perfect and as soon as he was, I took off running.

I sat up and took a deep breath. What was done was done. There was nothing left to do but leave. This would all heal and Michael and I would move on. If I'd made a horrible mistake I'd have to live with that. My wall was now completely rebuilt and I was out of tears for the day.

It was time to go home.

# CHAPTER TWENTY-FOUR

Everyone was awake and at the breakfast table when I returned to the house.

"Gwennie, where were you off to so early this morning?" my father said over his paper.

"What's this, Alice says you're leaving?" Mother chimed in. "We aren't heading home for another two weeks."

"I know, but I need to get back today," I said, quickly moving toward the stairs.

"Everything all right?" Simon asked, looking like he was going to get up.

"Fine! Really, I'm fine. I need to leave. Please enjoy your breakfast. I have a boat to catch." I ran up the stairs before Simon had a chance to get too close to me. I went into my room to make sure everything had been packed. Per usual, Alice was efficient and everything was waiting at the door.

Juan was right behind me. "Miss Gwen, Alice asked me to come and collect your things. The car is waiting outside to take you to the boat. We should probably hurry if you hope to make the morning crossing."

"Absolutely, Juan, I'm right behind you. Thank you for taking my bags. I need to be on that boat."

"Need? Something important at home?"

"Yes, I left myself there. Enough of this silly summer frolic, I have important things to do at home."

"I understand. It was lovely to meet you, Miss Gwen. Safe passage," Juan said as he opened the door to the waiting car.

"Nice meeting you, too. Thank you," I said, sounding very collected and in control.

The car pulled away from my parents' house as they waved to me and then disappeared behind the door, back to their breakfast. Driving toward the ship I felt nothing. I was numb. I'd escaped the house without an interrogation and, once I left the island, there would be no one at home who would even know of my summer on Catalina, or of Michael. I needed to make it to the boat; I'd erase all of this on the two-hour voyage home. I was in some sort of strange survival mode, like fight or flight. I'd read in several books that said animals have automatic instincts when threatened, that they have a split second where they decide to fight or fly away to safety. *Clearly I was flying*, I thought. *Get me to that boat.*

I tipped the driver, who handed my bags to the purser as I hurried onboard. Nothing was going to stand in my way. I didn't even wait to see if my bags made it safely onboard, nor did I stand to wave good-bye to the island as we pulled away. I sat on a bench to the side of the deck, with my back facing the island. I was done, on the boat, on my way home, and damaged. The passage was uneventful, probably because I didn't lift my eyes from my book the entire time. No deep breaths, glancing at my reflection, or feeling the wind in my face. I read the entire trip, but no matter how hard I tried to escape into the story in my lap, I couldn't. My story, my sad story, kept replaying in my mind. His scent, his eyes, and worst of all, his pain. Each mile away from the island should have made it easier, but there was no escaping.

As we pulled into Long Beach I looked over the rail and saw Rogers waiting for me. I was reminded of the day he dropped me off only a few months ago. I was so full of hope and total innocence. I was absurd. *Why did I fool myself into thinking one trip to Catalina would help me discover who I was and where I was going? I needed to sit down and take a hard look at myself. That was the only way to find answers.* I waited in my seat until most of the passengers had left the boat. My body didn't immediately get up. I was mentally stuck in my seat. I willed myself to make it to Rogers. Now walking down the stairs and past the empty luggage room I felt weak, as if part of me had been torn apart. I felt sick. I grabbed the railing as I made my way off the ship.

Rogers smiled as I approached. "Good to see you, Miss Gwen. I suppose you'll be carrying your own bags again?" I dropped my bags at my sides and began to cry like a child. Rogers was visibly taken aback and extended his large arms to embrace me. I moved past my bags and hugged him tightly. His jacket smelled of soap and cologne and his embrace felt familiar and warm. As my cheek pressed into his shoulder I continued to sob. Rogers took out his handkerchief and, without a word, gently pushed me back, dabbed my eyes, and handed it to me.

"Miss Gwen, I'm going to take you to the car and have the purser bring your bags behind us."

I said nothing; I followed Rogers to the car, sniffling and trying to keep myself from completely losing my composure.

I sat in the cool interior of the car and collapsed on the backseat. I lay down with my knees up on the bench seat. The car smelled familiar and I felt rescued and free to drop my guard, if only for the ride home. *I'd gone out into the world*, I thought, *and now I was back, beaten and bruised.* Because I'm not stupid, I knew I was in some sort of "oh, poor me" state, but right now it didn't feel like it was ever going to pass. My heart was broken, I was broken, and in pain. I was so grateful to be home. *Once I passed through the doors of the house I'd heal myself, rebuild.*

# CHAPTER TWENTY-FIVE

My first two weeks at home were a blur. They consisted mostly of eating, sleeping, and slouching around my parents' home. No one was expecting the family back from Catalina yet, so the house was silent except for Eudora, their other housekeeper, and Rogers, who, even though he was taking time off, insisted on being on call in case I needed anything. There was nothing I needed. At least, nothing either of them could give me. I spent my days roaming the house.

I looked through old scrapbooks in my father's office, read through old letters he'd written to my mother when they were courting. *Courting*, such a strange word, but in the context of my parents' letters, quite romantic. I had the run of the house and I used it to fully wallow in my pain and confusion. If I thought I lacked direction before Catalina, I was in real trouble now.

The day my parents were due to come home, Alice arrived to assist Eudora in preparing the house for their arrival. I stayed out of their way as they ran around dusting, cleaning, replenishing the kitchen, and ironing. Watching this whirlwind it came to me that I was wealthy...well, my parents were wealthy, so I was wealthy by association. I'd never really looked at it that way before. My parents' status always seemed like a trap I could fall into and wake up someone's bored, rich wife. But standing back that morning, having cried every tear left in me, I thought maybe my mother was right. I should accept my station in life, my place in society and just be…wealthy.

*Was that a life? Was there value there?* At the moment I didn't care. It seemed easy and I was looking for easy. I was sick of my self-righteous "do something with your life" attitude. I was wealthy and it was time I took advantage of the great privileges, as my mother called them. Wealth allowed for walls that would isolate me to exist with my own kind. There was no need to reach out and find real emotional connections anymore. I would hide behind a buffer and live on the surface. Surface I could do, surface was easy.

That morning I was done moping. I'd left Michael for a reason. Maybe there were times over the last couple of weeks my reasons seemed absurd. Maybe I was lying to myself and feeling I needed to figure out why I'd pushed him away, but now, on this morning, I was resolved. The pity party was over. I was young and wealthy. I'd focus on that. Live that life. *Finally, Gwen figures out what the hell she's going to do.* This would be easy. I ran upstairs to change. *I needed to call some old girlfriends. Not Mount Holyoke girls, but debutante girls. We needed to shop. I needed to prepare for my new life.*

# CHAPTER TWENTY-SIX

Helen and Elizabeth, from my cotillion days, promptly arrived at the house; they clearly had nothing else to do. The beauty of being the daughter in a wealthy family is there was never a shortage of available young ladies to call upon to go out on the town with. It was seen as constructively using your family connections. We were the prized ponies of the families in our circle. I was out prancing with the other ladies. I was slightly out of practice, but my reflexes returned quickly, owing to years of programming by my mother.

The secret about debutantes is they bore easily and are always looking for trouble. We're not our parents' young ladies. After the war some women came right out and declared themselves free and frisky, but the elite opted for short, bobbed hair and short skirts. We only wore rouge in private or dimly lit nightclubs. As for lipstick…well, we talked about those girls. This is what I ran from when I left for school, but here I was, and determined to take every advantage.

Helen Griever was my age and engaged to Thom Brandon. His parents own half of California, so she hit the jackpot. Unbeknownst to her family or her handsome but boring fiancé, Helen was having vertical rendezvous with the mechanic who worked on her father's Studebaker. I found out more about his washboard abs then I ever wanted to know over lunch. *So proud, she'll go on to do great things,*

I thought, trying to hear as little of the conversation as possible. Helen was a cliché and I smiled, nodded, and giggled with her and Lizzy. *This was no time to think.*

"Girls, we should go out and shake things up," I said after finishing my mimosa at the club. We'd shopped all afternoon and were now lunching.

"Yes! We should, they're having a social here next week. Unless you had something more serious in mind, and then we could head downtown to mingle with the common people," Lizzy said, as they both erupted in laughter and I, fighting back the vomit, joined in.

"Definitely downtown." I swallowed hard. "How about tomorrow night?"

"Perfect!" Helen winked at me. "So good to have you back with us, Gwennie. We've missed you." She finished with a little pouty-snuggle-face thing that she always did.

*This would work*, I thought as I slid my glasses on and climbed into the car waiting for me outside the club. I felt warm from just one drink and a little reckless. It felt great not to think. Arriving at my parents' house, I had the driver drop all of my shopping packages at the door.

"Alice," I called, in my very best spoiled-daughter-of-the-house voice.

"Hello, Miss Gwen," she said, walking into the entry. "Your parents are back and in the—"

"Yeah, great," I interrupted. "Please take these bags up to my room and put my new things away." She was staring at me in shock. "And Alice, please make sure you remove all of the tags. Not one tag, got it?" I flung my glasses on the entry table and dropped my coat on top of the bags. Alice stood there as I passed her. I felt a twinge of guilt, but I let it go. *This was the new and improved Gwen. These were the women that had everything they wanted and I was going to throw my life to hell and become one.*

I waltzed into the study, kissed my mother on both cheeks, much to her surprise, and hugged my father.

"Gwennie! So good to see you, sweetheart. You look great."

"You know, Dad, I feel great. I've come from the club." My father looked surprised.

"Really?" he asked.

"Yes, I shopped and lunched with Helen and Lizzy. Do you remember them? Boy, Lizzy's put on a little weight, huh, Mom?" My mother nodded a hesitant response and my father plopped into his chair, not quite sure what was going on.

"Gwendolyn, have you been drinking, dear?" Mother asked.

"A little but, boy, do I feel incredible. These last couple of weeks have been great for me. I've turned over a new leaf. The new and improved Gwen," I said, spreading my arms out to the both of them.

"What the hell was wrong with the old, no-frilly-top Gwen?" Father asked. "I liked her."

"Oh, Dad, you'll like this new version. I'm embracing my station and status in life. Mother…" I leaned down to my mother, who was now sitting on the couch, and whispered, "You won. I'm a socialite in the making. Helen and I had a lovely time. She told me about her fiancé and of course the grease monkey she's screw—"

"Gwendolyn!" Mother cut me off. "What has gotten into you? Collect yourself, please!"

"Ooh, sorry to offend, but so true." I put my finger over my lips to indicate a secret. I backed out of the study, looking at my father, who was stunned. *This is what you've always wanted, Mother.* The mimosa was wearing off and I was tired. My grin had faded. I looked both of them in the eye and went to my room. *My first day back in society and I felt…well, mission accomplished. I felt nothing at all.*

Weeks flew by filled with crew regattas, teas, and cocktails. I was living the life and, surprisingly, no one in my home really appreciated it. Turned out I heard more about the old Gwen than I had when she was around. My father was barely speaking to me, probably because we had little or nothing in common anymore. I was joining the ranks of the mindless and therefore missed out on the really good conversations. I was beginning to wonder if I was even capable of an intelligent conversation any longer.

In addition, Rogers informed me one evening after picking me up yet again at some stale, ridiculous party at the Mansion, a club in downtown Pasadena, that I was threatening my reputation hanging out in drinking clubs. I wanted to say that I didn't even drink, that I felt miserable enough without alcohol, but I was too tired to even care. *Imagine that, at twenty-four, living during Prohibition, and still threatening my reputation. I was good.* But nothing killed the pain. I still thought about Michael and most nights I fell asleep wondering if his life was the same hell I was living. All at once the questions came racing back. *What was I doing? Could I really keep this up forever? Marry some rich man and settle down?* I knew the answers; it would take me a few more months to find my way out.

# CHAPTER TWENTY-SEVEN

The holidays were a whirlwind. The annual Tournament of the Roses Parade and the Rose Bowl were rapidly approaching. Mother is on the board, so she was busy with planning and luncheons. I helped and actually enjoyed the history that went along with the parade. I was beginning to think again. *That would have to stop.* At the breakfast table, Mother was addressing invitations to her annual Rose Bowl Brunch and Party. Everyone would arrive for brunch and stay for the game. Kickoff was at 2:10 sharp. I'd heard my father say, "Georgia Tech against Cal this year, so it ought be a good one." I wasn't well versed in football, but I was good at licking envelopes, so I sat at the table with Mother, had tea, and helped her.

"Mother, what's this?" I held up one of the envelopes, clearly addressed to Mr. Cathner and family.

"Let me see, dear…oh, your father wanted me to invite Frank and his son…" she said, trailing off.

"Michael?" I said it quickly; to ease the sting. "Michael is coming to your brunch?" There was a hint of panic in my voice.

"Well, they haven't even received the invitation yet, so I'm not sure." She was uncomfortable. "It was your father's idea, so don't get all ruffled with me." I sealed the envelope and put it into a pile with the others. *He wouldn't come. It was over and there was no way to get me back. I didn't want him back. I was well into my new life.* I sat drinking my tea, sure he hated me and he would surely not like what I'd become—or maybe he would. *Stop it, Gwen, here you go again.*

I excused myself from the table and went to my room. I wanted to read today and be alone.

The new year arrived, as did the Tournament of Roses Parade in all its pageantry. Mother's party was a rousing success and I listened to my parents' friends and Simon's friends discuss how the poor center for Cal ran the wrong way and lost the game to the Yellow Jackets from Georgia. I partied up to my new reputation, and as I expected, Michael did not arrive. Father had mentioned they declined the invitation because they were working feverishly to finish the casino for the opening in May. As the guests were leaving, Simon and I sat out back on the swings we played on as children. I'd exhausted myself doing absolutely nothing and I was feeling that I'd reached the end of my shelf life as a Roaring Twenties party girl. I wanted to return to the days of these swings. Start over, be a child again. I wasn't sure what I'd do differently, but I knew, sitting there, I was unhappy.

"You all right?" Simon asked as he spun on his swing to face me.

"Me? Oh yeah, I'm really great," I said, giving him a sugary grin.

"I'm serious, when're you going to stop this? You're obviously in pain. Please stop. Believe me, sis, this doesn't work. I've tried. There isn't enough flirting or alcohol to get rid of the ache." I stared at the ground, making myself dizzy. Simon gently lifted my chin and wiped the eyeliner that was drifting down my face.

"Sis, you love him. There's nothing you can do about it. And guess what? He's a great guy and he desperately loves you, too. What're the two of you doing?"

I began to cry. "I can't. I'm scared. What if I wake up and I hate him, or even worse, I hate myself?"

"This is better? You don't even have what you had before you met him. What's going to be left of you? You can make it work with him. Why's everything so black and white with you?"

"This is temporary. I'm coming out of this. I'll be back to myself in no time. I need to get back on track. I had plans before. I need to find them again..." My head was throbbing. "But right now, I need to go to bed." Simon helped me to my room and kissed me on the cheek as he brought me toward the bed.

"I love you, sis," he whispered as I lay down.

"I love you, too, little brother," I mumbled back as I rolled over and drifted to sleep.

# CHAPTER TWENTY-EIGHT

The next morning as my head pulsed resting on my pillow, I made a decision. I was still a wealthy debutante, but I no longer partied. *At least for a while. This couldn't continue.* I felt awful. I needed a hobby. It was time to emerge and start doing something with myself. I poured my body into the bathtub and thought about my options. I could ask my mother if there were any boards or societies that needed help. *Why*? I thought. I was college educated. What did I want to do for the rest of my life? So I'd arrived back to the original question that brought me to Catalina. *Still no answer, great!*

I broke down what I knew for certain. I wanted to be a doctor. I majored in biology; I loved the idea of being in medicine. I needed to see the realities of medicine, see if it was where I'd make my career. Wrapping myself in a towel, I decided I'd go down to the Pasadena Hospital and see what opportunities there were for me. I'd pull myself out of this. A debutante I may appear to the outside world, but I'd have a secret identity: Elizabeth Blackwell. Brushing my hair and getting dressed, I felt better already. No makeup today; I would give it a rest for the day. I grabbed my bag and headed to breakfast.

"Well, good morning, sis," Simon said from behind his paper. He and Father were reading side by side, like bookends, and discussing the ups and downs of the stock market. Putting the paper down he said, "You look…well, you look great. Occasion?"

"I'm going down to the hospital this morning to see what kinds of opportunities they have available for bright, articulate girls like myself." We both laughed. It had been a while since I'd laughed. It felt good.

I kissed Simon on the forehead. "Thanks!" He knew everything that *thanks* meant. *Thank you for being my brother. Thank you for telling me exactly what I needed to hear.*

"You're quite welcome. Go get 'em!"

It was a crisp January morning, a new year. Pasadena Hospital was a small hospital about as old as I was. As a matter of fact, I was born in this hospital when it was only four years old. It seemed appropriate I would return at another pivotal stage in my life.

The staff was busy, but very helpful. I was put in touch with the clinical coordinator and they had a premed program for students looking to go to medical school. This was exactly what I needed. After a couple of weeks, some paperwork, and several interviews, I became the newest member of their program, going on rounds with physicians, helping at the nurses' stations—I was even able to view a surgery. I began to come alive; my drive returned.

I'd been at the hospital a little over a month, going out only with Simon again and reading voraciously anything I could get my hands on about medicine. I felt myself emerging. I was going to be fine. I still thought of Michael every day, mostly wanting to share what I was learning with him, but I was proud of myself again. Besides, he knew where I lived. He must have moved on.

It was a Sunday, my day off, and I sat at the table with my father, sharing the paper. Herbert Hoover was our new president and, while Father still waited for an end to Prohibition, or as he put it, "The damn government sticking their nose in my whisky cabinet," he liked that Hoover was a Republican. We had things to talk about again and that felt great.

"So how are things going at the hospital?" he asked.

"Good...great, actually."

"Terrific, it's really growing down there. I hear they have two surgery rooms now?"

"They do, how'd you know...you're on the board, aren't you?" I shook my head and smiled at him.

"I'm the newest member of the Pasadena Hospital board. Guilty. I like to keep an eye on my girl. They have nothing but great things to say about you, as expected. So, medical school?" he asked.

"I don't know yet. I'm really happy doing what I'm doing."

"Good...good. You know they just bought the Catalina Island Hospital? The board did—big plans to expand and update the hospital on the island," my father said, peeking over his paper, smiling at me.

"Really?" I smiled back. "Well, that facility needs it, so that's good, good. Daddy, you didn't have anything to do with that purchase, did you?" I glared at him.

"I don't know what you're talking about. You said the facility needed a lot of work, so it was a logical move for the investors. I presented the information and they were smart enough to do something about it." He never lowered the paper, but I imagined him snickering like a little boy.

My mother came to the table with yet another set of invitations. I gave her a look that said, "You're sending invitations again?"

She looked at me and smiled. "What? Easter brunch. These need to go out at least a month in advance. Are you volunteering your licker again?" She giggled at herself.

"Sure, why not." I smiled. The invitation list was much larger than the Rose Bowl party. My mother's Easter brunch was famous. We had relatives come in from all over the country to join in her festivities. Two hundred eggs for the children to find. It was crazy and I usually had dye on my fingers for a month afterward from all of the egg-dyeing the night before. This year I was looking forward to it. I was finding peace in the traditions of my family.

"Simon dressing up as the Easter Bunny again?" I asked.

"He most certainly is. Isn't he, John?" She looked at my father.

He laughed from behind the paper. "I'm sure he is—it seems to be the only steady job Simon can hold on to." Lowering the paper, he smiled warmly at my mother. We all laughed. The invitations were beautiful and again *the* envelope came across my pile.

"Again? Why?" I asked them both.

"Cathners?" my father asked, hidden behind the newsprint, again.

"Yes, why do you continue to invite them?"

"Oh, they're already coming. I spoke to Frank this morning. They'll be in town for last-minute things before the casino opening, so they'll be here," he said nonchalantly, but still hiding.

I said nothing. I looked at my mother.

"That's great. I'll put the two of them down," Mother said, completely oblivious, or pretending to be completely oblivious.

"I think there'll be three of them," he mumbled.

"Three," I said.

"That's what Frank said."

"All right then, three it is," Mother said, continuing to hand me more envelopes.

*He's coming to my house in a month. Thirty short days and he'll be here. OK, I can handle this. I'm back on track and if there're three of them, he's probably bringing a date. Even better—we've both moved on.* I took a deep breath and decided I would take my mother's lead and pretend for a while.

# CHAPTER TWENTY-NINE

Thirty short days buzzed by and I was standing in front of the mirror in my bedroom. Guests would begin arriving any minute. I needed to get downstairs and start helping. *Yes, that was it. Keep busy and everything will work itself out.*

The rooms downstairs looked beautiful, perfect. My mother was really good at this—warm, so warm. *Happy Easter! Here we go.* I helped take coats in the beginning and then moved to mingling with the guests. Robert arrived with his parents, looking great and relaxed in his Easter colors.

"You look fabulous, Gwen," he said, grabbing a mimosa.

"Well, you do, too," I said, flirting a little. Robert was fun to flirt with because I knew it would never go anywhere, at least not for me. Simon began walking toward me with a look on his face, and suddenly I couldn't breathe.

I knew he was there even before I turned around. I just knew. Gathering my strength I slowly glanced toward the double doors. The breath streamed slowly from my lips and there were his eyes, gazing at mine for a moment while he feigned conversation with some stunning woman on his arm. My stoic stare began to soften as I turned to face my other guest. *Pull it together, Gwen, you're on your turf and clearly he has moved on.*

"Well—" Robert's voice broke my trance. "Gwen?"

"Um, I'm sorry, what were you saying?"

"Did you enjoy the rest of your summer? How's the casino?" Robert asked, slightly impatient with my distraction.

"Yes…yes, the rest of the summer was beautiful and it was so good to see you on the island. Simon was happy to see you and yes, I hear the casino is almost finished. Father has been back a couple of times and I hear it's quite a sight. Robert, are you joining everyone in a couple of weeks back on the island for the casino's big opening night?" I asked, looking straight into his eyes, hoping to make amends.

"I'll be there. Simon tells me you won't? You'll be sorely missed."

"I—I can't. I'm working at the hospital and can't get away. I'm sure it will be wonderful." I smiled, feeling more and more uneasy. I could feel Michael in the room, but I couldn't look at him without seeming obvious.

"I really love that island, so I'm sure we'll have a superb time." He smiled, putting his empty champagne glass on a passing silver tray. "Will you excuse me, Gwen? I must chat with my parents."

"Absolutely," I said, gently touching his hand as he crossed in front of me.

I walked purposefully across the drawing room, behind the newly upholstered couch to the window by the largest of the brunch tables. I ran my finger along the crisp, white linens, pretending to inspect the spread. The glasses glistened in the sunlight spraying in from the back windows. This home was perfect in the afternoon. Muted yellows and ivory from the rugs to the moldings, all illuminated by the midday sun. A warm, early summer breeze drifted in, caressing the sheer curtains and circulating the smell of wood and lavender. I closed my eyes by the window and allowed the warmth to wash over my face. *This is my world*, I thought. *This is where I belong and I'm fine. I can get past seeing him. It no longer affects my life.*

I felt a slight push at my back as a hand, his hand, gently pressed the curve of my body. I kept my eyes closed and, in spite of myself, I was transported back to the island, before it all fell apart. His body was close to me and his scent created a melodic sensation right through me. *This man was…even with my eyes closed he was overwhelming.* I slowly opened my eyes.

"Hello, Gwen," he said softly into the back of my neck.

"Michael, when did you arrive?" I mumbled, pathetically trying to be coy.

"You saw me arrive. Are you going to turn around?" He asked, still with one hand discreetly on my back.

"No." I said softly. "Please…walk away. Head back to your date," I said, not turning from the window.

"She's a friend," he clarified. "Did you expect me to come alone?"

"I didn't expect anything." I took a deep breath, made sure my wall was firmly in place, and then I turned toward him. Taking his hand by the wrist I said, "I need you to take your hand off me. Listen, Michael, it's nice of you to visit my parents while you're here and… Happy Easter, but I've moved on." My heart was pounding out of my chest. "Please don't walk up to me like we're friends. You are—were a distraction that has been over for some time. What was it you said? 'There's another one coming in on the next boat?' I'm home now and you and I…" I stopped when I saw the obvious pain in his face.

"Are finished. Right. Probably a good thing you won't be at the casino opening," he replied, softly but coldly.

"I see no point in going back there. Robert and I are heading back east for a little visit." I smiled, taking another glass of champagne from the table. *Lie, Gwen.*

"You and Robert, huh. Is he really—"

"Perfect? He sure is." I sipped a little more bubbly, and in my worst performance of the day, threw my head back and feigned a laugh. *Was he seeing through this? His smell was intoxicating. His lips, his eyes, I couldn't even look in his eyes.* The entire rush of him returned instantly. It had only been a few months, but it seemed like an eternity since I'd touched Michael, since I'd broken my own heart. I needed to get through this. *It was too late for us.* If he didn't hate me when he arrived, he would now.

"Perfect. Well, it doesn't get any better than that, now does it?" Michael smiled. He looked into my eyes. My body went numb. "So, you and Robert are a…couple?" The sarcasm was thick. *You're losing, Gwen, do something.*

"We run in the same social circles. I've dated quite a few of his friends since I've been back, but we have a real connection."

"Really, social circles, huh. Well, that's fabulous, Miss Ross!" There it was, the mocking I was waiting for. I paused for the final bite and then it arrived.

"Who the hell are you? Are you happy, Gwen? This is what you've reduced yourself to…a tipsy debutante trophy for the likes of Robert and his cronies to pass around the social circle?" Michael was angry and definitely in pain. "Wow, I've been with a lot of women like you, but I had no idea the caliber of woman—no, socialite—I was dealing with when we met." He was standing so close to me I could feel his breath on my cheek as I tried to look away. He was talking into my neck and it took every bit of energy I had to keep from dropping my champagne glass. "Miss Ross, so sorry to have bothered you with my silly island-boy drivel. I'll leave you alone now."

I blinked back the swell building in my eyes and turned back toward the window. I wanted to say, "No, I've found myself again. I'm the woman you're in love with, but I'm scared to death." I had no breath and I began to quietly gasp for air. I felt the shoulder of his jacket brush my back as he turned and walked away.

"Mr. Cathner," a familiar voice boomed from behind me.

"Rob, how are you? Sportin' the sandals even off the island, I see."

"Well, you know a woman once told me I had beautiful feet," Robert replied with a chuckle.

"Really? Hmm…" Michael said with a hint of sarcasm. He was on his best behavior and even with my back turned I could tell he held back so as not to offend.

"How long you on the mainland? Shouldn't you be back finishing up the entryway to the casino? I hear you're cutting it pretty close." *Oh, please, Rob. Please stop!*

"Rob," Michael began to reply, but Robert interrupted him.

"Let's use 'Robert' now that we're home, shall we?"

*Oh, this wasn't happening.* Still looking out the window, I prayed I would somehow disappear.

"All right, Robert…well, happy Easter to you…Sam and Joe are finishing up the entry and we're right on schedule," Michael replied. "I came to the mainland to pick up some supplies and do some shopping for the big opening. Mr. and Mrs. Ross were kind enough to invite us to share in their Easter celebration, so if you don't mind, I'm taking a little break." There was tension in his voice now. "Believe me, I can't wait to get back." That last part was for my benefit and I could feel Michael's stare.

"Great, well, I can't wait to see it," Rob replied.

"See what?"

"The finished casino, of course."

"You're going to the opening?"

"Wouldn't miss it." I was sure Rob was smiling his best vaudeville smile.

"But I thought you and…" I could feel him turn to me and I wanted to die. How could I have made up a lie and not included Rob? *Stupid, Gwen, really stupid.*

Michael let out a slight laugh, "Ah, of course…never mind. Well, we'll see you on the island, then."

I fixed my eyes on the window and tried to casually sip more champagne. I couldn't turn around. If I turned around the whole room would know what Michael already knew. I loved him.

*I didn't say it that night in Catalina, but he knew and he knows now. That's why he's here. That's why he brought that beautiful woman with him. He's pretending he's moved on and he's looking for a reaction. He needs to know that I'm not the cold, heartless woman who left him standing there with his heart in his hand. He wants to believe I didn't throw away everything we had over one night of drunken comments made among friends at the Tuna Club. He believes in me, and he knows this whole front I'm putting on is just that, a front. I let him in on that island, way in, and now he's come to claim me. Rescue me from the clutches of the pathetic fortress that I've built for myself. But once again I'd managed to push him away. Go back to the island, Michael.*

I put my glass on the table, turned quickly without looking at anyone, and left the room. Once out of sight I ran to my room, threw myself on the bed, and cried. *Why wouldn't this go away? How was I ever going to get over him? Why would anyone want to get over him?*

# CHAPTER THIRTY

Surprised I'd not been awakened earlier, I intentionally decided to stay in my pajamas. I slouched down the stairs, hoping for some kind of breakfast roll and tea I could take back to my room. I didn't want to see anyone; I wanted to be alone in my misery. It was already eleven o'clock, so I was sure my parents were out and about, tending to their Monday chores. Any holdover guests from the festivities were long gone by now, heading back to their own fabulous homes and all-important social calendars.

Alice greeted me as I pushed through the white double doors of the kitchen. Alice is a small woman, but hearty, and she was seated, reading a magazine. She stood immediately, not sure which Gwen she was going to get today. I'd brought back the nasty Gwen for Michael last night, but that Gwen was gone this morning. *Who was I kidding? Michael was right. Who the hell was I?* More confused than ever, I felt absurd and…

"Miss Gwen? You're still here? Are you all right? You look awful," she said, trying to figure me out.

"Thank you, Alice." I laughed at her honesty. I needed someone to be honest with me.

"I didn't mean that…you don't look yourself," she said, trying to soften the blow. "I don't think I've ever seen you in your pajamas this late, ma'am, even when you were a child. Is everything all right?"

"Great, just...fantastic!" I said flashing a corny smile and opening the icebox. I felt crazy, like one of those people wandering the halls of a mental hospital.

"Miss Gwen, can I make you some breakfast or...lunch?" Alice asked, looking a little nervous.

"Alice, I'd like a roll, a breakfast roll or something left over from brunch. You know what? I'd like a whole darn basket of rolls. Yes, and a pot of tea with milk and sugar on the side and one of those pretty napkins you put with it. Do you know the ones I mean?" I said, holding both of her shoulders gently to keep her from buzzing around me. Alice stared at me, nodding with every word I said. "Can you get that for me, Alice?"

"Yes, ma'am. I'll put it all together for you and bring it to the dining room. Why don't you have a..."

"Nope, I'll have it in...my...room!" I interrupted.

"Your room?" she asked, pulling down a tray and teapot.

"Yes, please," I said over my shoulder, walking toward the kitchen doors and grabbing a handful of grapes from the fruit bowl sitting on the cutting block.

"Alice." I turned at the door. "Thank you and...I'm sorry I was such a..." I wasn't sure what to call my behavior. "I've lost my mind, Alice, and I'm sorry." I wanted to cry, but my eyes were dry and burning.

"Miss Gwen...please...you're...fine. You don't owe me an apology." Alice was now very uncomfortable, and had propriety allowed her, she would've hugged me. Instead, she said, "There isn't anything I wouldn't do for you, Miss Gwen. You're an incredible young lady, but you're still young. Give things some time. Please stop being so hard on yourself. It's painful to watch." With that, Alice had given me her thoughts. She reached out to me with her words and embraced me. "Go put your feet up and get some rest. I'll be right up," she finished.

Pushing through both doors, letting them swing behind me, I made my grand exit. I was feeling sorry for myself today. I'd spent yesterday avoiding the eyes and touch of the man I loved, and today I would be the guest of honor at yet another pity party. I didn't care about a single formality or obligation, not today. Gwen the debutante was dead, and I was happy to kiss her good-bye, as I'm sure everyone around me was.

Alice brought up the tray and put it on the table in my room. She gave me what I had asked for, including a beautiful linen napkin and even some fresh flowers. I walked over to the tray as she said, "Miss Gwen, this was left for you yesterday. Thrown on the entry table as one of the guests left." I looked down at her hand and saw the beautiful script I knew so well spelling my name on the envelope.

"You can leave it there. Thank you, Alice," I said, as she placed the envelope on the tray and walked toward the door.

Looking at me she said, "Handsome man, Mr. Cathner."

"Yes, yes, I suppose he is. Thank you, Alice."

"Let me know if you need anything else," she said and then she was gone.

I looked over at the letter from Michael, beckoning me to open it. Whatever words were on that paper, I was sure I had them coming to me. What more could he say that wasn't fired at me yesterday? Had he written it before he came? Maybe he wrote it after we'd talked yesterday. Perhaps there were more bitter, angry words that would free me from this crushing pain. This letter—the final blow—would finish it and I would know it was over. I held the envelope in my hands, took a deep breath, and pulled out the letter:

*The greatest tragedy of life is not that men perish, but that they cease to love.*

—W. Somerset Maugham

That's how his letter began and it continued…

Dearest Gwen—

You have broken my heart into a million pieces. I tried to retreat in pain back to the man I was before I met you and I have failed. You never really left the island. You are everywhere I go. Every place on the island has become a painful memory. There is neither a drink nor another woman that can heal this hurt.

Following what seemed like eternity after you left, the sun began to shine again and I realized I don't want to be the man I was before I met you. I want to always see myself the way I was in the reflection of your eyes.

Please accept my heartfelt apology for my stupid antics at the Tuna Club that night. Believe me, it was innocent banter and not meant to hurt or belittle you or what we had together. I'm sure it wasn't easy to hear me acting like an idiot, but I'm not perfect. I never pretended to be perfect. I understood your anger, but you used that as a reason to run.

What we have scares you. It scares me too; never again will I love a woman the way I love you, Gwen. I'm certain of that. I was moving past my fear because I couldn't imagine living without you. I adore you, everything about you. I would never want to change one thing. We were just getting started and I'm sorry for the hurtful things I said the morning you left, but my life was over when you walked out.

I miss you every morning and every night and I'm afraid I will do so for the rest of my life. I'm writing this as I get ready to go to your parents' home. I'm sure you will be there. My heart is racing at the mere thought of seeing you. I come alive when I'm near you; the warmth will return to my body, if only for a moment. I'm not sure what will happen when I see you this afternoon, but I wanted to write this either way. Also, let me say up front that my date is there as a distraction to numb the pain. You have probably retreated to your world and moved past me.

Gwen, I wish you much happiness and pray that you are not living with the same ache that has become my every moment. I will love you all my life. I've heard that you are not planning to attend the casino opening. I'm writing to ask you to attend as one last favor to me. It's an important night and I would like for you to be there. Please come back to the island for only one night and then I'll leave you to your life; you have my word.

Yours always,
Michael

The letter dropped to my feet as my whole body began to throb and I crumpled onto the bed. There it was again, the pain, or ache, as Michael so aptly put it. The worst sting was the thought of what Michael and I could have been. That was the most painful part. *What if I'd trusted him? Told him he was a jerk at the Tuna Club? Gone with my heart? Where would we be now? We could have avoided all of the ugly words the day I left the island and the even uglier scene yesterday. Was it the fairy tale and I walked away?* I couldn't take it anymore. With my pillow damp beneath my face, I pulled the covers up and did what I thought impossible. I cried again.

# CHAPTER THIRTY-ONE

The next morning, Mother knocked on my door to invite me to lunch and some shopping. This was a big step, because we'd only spoken when necessary for the last few weeks, and now lunch? *She wanted something.*

Alice came in my room to put some things away and clear my tray from yesterday. I'd locked my door last night, so she hadn't been able to clear it then, which I knew didn't mesh well with her need for order.

"So, I'm going to lunch with my mother," I said, knowing Alice would see the oddity of my situation.

"Well, that's nice. I'm sure you'll have a lovely time. I know Mrs. Ross was on the phone this morning with Mrs. Platt from the island. Maybe she worked up an appetite," she said. This was Alice code. She'd heard something, but it went against her sense of propriety to snoop, so she hinted instead.

"Mrs. Platt? What were they talking about?"

"I couldn't hear everything. I mean, I wasn't listening, but it was quite a long conversation," Alice said, making the bed. "Your mother did sound very concerned and they were talking about you and, well, the things you've been going through. Mrs. Platt must've been talking highly of you, because your mother kept saying, 'I know she's a wonderful girl.'"

"She said that? Are you sure?" Alice nodded. "Miss Gwen, your mother loves you a great deal. I know she can be…difficult, but I know…I see her when you're not looking, when you're not here. She cares a great deal. Do you know she spent months putting together this room for you? She wouldn't let anyone else do a thing."

I stared at Alice in shock. My mother was complicated, but then again, so was I. As I got older, I was realizing that I might be part of the problem in my relationship with my mother. In my youth, I went out of my way to get at her. There was something about her orderly life I wanted to destroy as a child, and even recently. She wasn't a bad person, and I'd never really bothered to get to know her. Maybe it was that simple—I needed to get to know her and all would be well? *Seems way too easy.*

We drove into town. I'd anticipated my mother would enjoy my return to society, but as I found out that afternoon, she liked me the way I was. That was good, because I liked the old me, too. We lunched at the club, and Mother started in right away.

"What has happened to you, Gwendolyn?" *Take a deep breath, Gwen. Maybe what she means is "I'm worried about you."*

"Mother, I'm finding my way."

"You seemed so full of life and promise on Catalina. Stubborn as all bulls, but alive. You look lost inside. There's no one home in your eyes." I began to tear up as she continued, "You know, dear, I always wanted you to embrace your status and position in this family, because it was safer for you. But I know the dark side to this world and the double lives that a lot of these girls live. It wasn't like that when I was a girl. Sure, we had your occasional scandal, but nothing like it is now. I wanted you to grow up to be a young lady and marry a nice man. Is that so wrong? Maybe I pushed it too much, but I didn't want you wandering around. I was talking to Mrs. Platt this morning, and she just went on and on about how wonderful you are and how she sees so much potential in you." For a minute I thought maybe my mother had decided she liked me because the all-knowing Mrs. Platt liked me. *There is no way she is that shallow. Besides, there is more in her eyes today.*

"But, this...well, this is all wrong for you. You're so bright, Gwen, and...I know...I know I never put much value on that, and I know you don't understand me, but I..." She took my hands, and, in a gesture that was so out of her comfort area it brought me to tears, she raised my hands to her lips and kissed them. "I love you, sweetheart. I know that I don't show it well, but I don't want to lose you to something you don't want. You've lost your sparkle, and your father and I are very worried about you. The hospital is a good thing for you, but at Easter you..." I gently pulled my hands away.

I put the starched napkin up to my eyes to try to avoid completely losing it. I couldn't stop crying, so I held the napkin there for a minute. I expected to look over and see my mother looking around the room to see who was witnessing my scene, but she wasn't. She was looking at me lovingly. She was worried, and I loved her for it, but there was nothing she could do. Our salads arrived, and she continued, "Your father thinks this has to do with Michael, the boy from the island, the boy at Easter?" She buttered her bread as if we were talking about the weather. His name hung in the air between us like a forbidden fruit. She'd never mentioned his name before. Now here we were discussing him as if he was a friend of the family.

"I don't want to discuss this, Mother. I'm finding my way."

"You know, I loved your father something fierce when we first met. I wasn't sure he loved me as much as I loved him. Of course, he grew to love me, but when we first met, I was head over heels." I ate my salad wondering where this was going. Had this conversation with Mrs. Platt jogged something loose? "He was beautiful and so charming, exactly like he is now, minus the belly and the gray hair." She laughed at herself and spoke of my father as if he were straight out of a fantasy. *He was. I'd known it my whole life. He was perfect.*

"But he wasn't always the man you know today, sweetheart. He took some getting used to, and he had a wandering eye that broke my heart a couple of times while we were dating." Mother put her napkin in her lap as the waiter removed her salad. "Gwendolyn, no man is perfect. Your father wasn't, and neither is this Michael person. You wouldn't want him to be." I was stunned by this honesty. My mother was opening up to me, and I didn't know what to say.

"Did Daddy ever cheat on you?"

"No, absolutely not, but he liked the ladies when we were dating. I wondered if I was enough. I loved him so much in the beginning, and I was certain something would spoil it. Mainly me. I was worried I'd spoil it." She smiled at me, looking for a reaction.

"I'd no idea. You always seem like you're better than he is, that you elevate him to his perfection."

"Oh, dear, we elevate each other. Your father taught me about myself. I learned to see myself not only through my critical eyes, but through his adoring eyes, too. He does the same thing. We feed off each other. That's a good relationship."

"But you're so different."

"We are, but why on earth would I want to be with someone exactly like me? Where is the fun in that?"

"You like to have fun?"

"Gwendolyn, of course I like to have fun. I just don't find myself tipsy in the bathroom stalls of nightclubs." She rolled her eyes, and we laughed. Like mother and daughter we laughed, and I felt less alone. I looked at my mother. She was flawed and human. I would remember this day and the strength my mother showed and gave to me for the rest of my life.

# CHAPTER THIRTY-TWO

I'd made arrangements to be away from the hospital for a while and decided to return to Catalina for the casino opening. The whole family was going and was quite excited. Mary and George were meeting us over there. The baby was staying with George's parents. According to my mother, Mary and George were adjusting to having the baby and seemed happy. They were working at being a couple. It was so nice to hear they were happy.

Father, Mother, Simon, and I arrived at the boat terminal to return to the island. Rogers opened the door and extended his hand yet again to help me out of the car.

"Thank you," I said, feeling overwhelmed by everything Rogers meant in my life.

"You're very welcome, Miss Ross. May I help you with your bags?"

"You may. I'll carry these bags, but would you please take the others and get me checked in?" I said, looking into his eyes. I'd grown up. I no longer needed to prove myself with the bags. Rogers understood and began collecting my bags.

"Rogers?"

"Yes, ma'am?"

"I'll get my own coffee, though."

"Very well," he said with a chuckle.

"Rogers?"

"Ma'am?"

"I've loved you my whole life. Thank you." I dropped my bags and hugged him with both arms. I held him tight.

"I've loved you your entire life, too, Miss Gwen, and you're quite welcome. It's been my pleasure." He smiled at me, looking a little choked up himself.

"All right, enough of 'hug Rogers.' Let's get checked in," Simon interrupted, and then he moved toward Rogers as if he were going to kiss him. Rogers put up his fist, and they both laughed.

The boat trip over was wonderful. I felt at peace. I was with people I loved, and I felt free to tell them so. I'd been through a lot this year, and I'd dealt with some of my demons. I didn't feel afraid. I was going back to Catalina, and whatever happened, I would be fine. I knew who Gwendolyn Ross was, or at least I knew who she was at twenty-five. I knew what I wanted to do for right now, and that was enough as the sea air caressed my face. I looked at myself in the glass reflection behind me. I was quite pretty. I was older, and I liked what I saw in the reflection, exactly as I was.

Catalina presented herself to us, and we were back. She was beautiful, and the casino was magnificent, even from the boat. A one-of-a-kind masterpiece, perfect for this incredible place. I gathered my things and ran toward Avalon. I was home; my heart was home. My parents had sent Alice ahead, and the house was ready for us when we arrived. Everything was exactly as I'd left it. I climbed the stairs to my room. So much had happened in this house. I was filled with memories as I opened the door. This was where I had spent so many dream-filled nights falling in love. I allowed myself to remember, which was something I'd not allowed since I'd run from the island. I lay on the bed and breathed it all in. All of it, the good and the not so good. I closed my eyes and tucked all of these memories away. They would always be a part of me, a good part of me. I started to unpack my clothes. I had no regrets.

# CHAPTER THIRTY-THREE

That evening, looking out the window of my room, I felt the beads of my dress touch my toes as I slid the peach-colored gown onto my body. The lights from the boats below danced on the harbor, and the glow coming from the casino was unlike anything I'd ever seen. It was magical, like a castle in a far-off land. Alice fastened the tiny buttons on the back of my dress as I turned toward the mirror and my dressing table.

"You look so beautiful, Miss Gwen. Like a princess."

"Thank you," I said, in a voice much softer than my normal voice. *It must be the dress,* I thought. I stared at myself in the mirror as Alice handed me my earrings. *I do look beautiful—tall, and my neck looks long and graceful,* I thought. Of course, I was standing still. It was always the moving part that ruined my graceful image, but for now, I looked like a swan version of myself.

"Are you excited, ma'am?"

"To see the casino?"

"To see everything," Alice said, not so subtly.

"I'm here, and yes, I'm excited for the opening of the casino, Alice. Michael and I…well, it seems too late for that, and I'm really fine. This will be a sensational night."

Alice smiled as she touched up my hair, which was pulled up and back on one side, loosely forming a nest of curls fastened with little diamond clips shaped like butterflies. *How appropriate,* I thought, remembering the day Michael and I had spent in the interior of the island, his breath mixing with mine as he rescued a butterfly from my hair. *Yes, quite appropriate.*

Of course, that day had ended in an argument, and I was hoping this evening would be peaceful and bring some closure. Michael had said this was one last favor, and I was free to live my life. I would figure out how to do that without him as soon as this evening was over. I brushed a curl from my face and took a full look at myself. My hair and nails were compliments of Fern, the beautician in town Mother had hired to fluff us up. Mother was beaming and so excited to show off her family.

I pursed my lips and felt different—grown, hurt, and yes, beautiful. I was looking at a full woman in the mirror. My time on the island had given me so much, and this felt like the perfect ending. Learning to work and compromise, leaving my safe, comfortable shelter and going out into the world. I was wiser and stronger. I pulled my shoulders back, put my gloves on, and took my bag from Alice, who kissed me on both cheeks and opened the door to my room.

I walked down the hallway to the stairs and, to my surprise, floated down the staircase exactly as I'd always rehearsed in my mind. Years of socials and my latest stint as a reformed debutante and I'd finally gotten it right. My very dapper brother was standing at the foot of the stairs with his mouth visibly open.

"You're…wow!"

"I'll take that as a compliment," I said, poking him.

"Gwen, you're beautiful," he said, kissing me on the cheek.

"You too, Simon."

My mother and father came around the corner from the dining area, looking the image of perfection, with the exception of my father's crooked bow tie, which mother promptly fixed.

"Gwennie, you're gorgeous as always, honey."

"Thanks, Dad," I replied, kissing him and waiting for some comment as my mother approached.

Straightening my shoulders and then gently touching my cheek, my mother leaned into my ear and whispered, "Love agrees with you, sweetheart." She smiled that warm, motherly smile that I'd been seeing a lot of lately. I was given another glimpse into her window of sunlight that was normally closed off. I was again grateful. With that gesture, she turned to my father, and we were ready.

"Where are Mary and George?" my father said as we walked through the door to the car waiting outside.

"They're meeting us there," Mother replied, climbing into the car.

# CHAPTER THIRTY-FOUR

The air was crisp and the ocean was thrashing against the breakwater as we emerged to walk the carpet laid out for the opening. Simon extended his hand to help me out of the car and gently looped my arm around his. My heart began to race as I looked up at the billowing panels of material covering the murals on the outside of the casino. There was just enough breeze to tussle with some pretty elaborate hairstyles. I could hear the sound of the orchestra spilling out through the arched windows above. The evening was extraordinary, and I was now officially nervous. A tall gentleman in black tie and tails ushered us to a grassy area where all the guests were gathering and enjoying hors d'oeuvres and refreshments.

"Good evening, Mr. and Mrs. Ross, Miss Ross, Mr. Ross. We will be unveiling the murals on the outside of the casino in approximately fifteen minutes and then opening the main entrance for dancing and dinner. Thank you for coming, and enjoy your evening."

Simon and I followed my parents over to a large roped-off area with a lovely bar and waiters in starched vests carrying silver trays. My sister, Mary, and her husband, George, were looking at each other lovingly in an area toward the back. They'd been through a lot this year, and it looked as if George was able to show Mary she was the only woman for him. Their relationship seemed happier since it had fallen apart and they had rebuilt it.

"Mary, you're lovely," I said, kissing my sister. "George, always nice to see you."

"And you—" Mary said, holding my hands out to the side and taking in a full view. "You're all grown up, little sister, and quite lovely yourself."

Mary and I had never been what I would call close, but it seemed we were united in some kind of womanhood that night. We could not be more different, but at that moment we seemed to have more in common. I cherished the look on her face and hugged her again.

"May I have everyone's attention?" An announcer's voice boomed from the front of the casino. Everyone moved toward the main entrance for the unveiling of the murals.

"I heard they were still finishing these this morning," I heard one woman say. "Do we know what the murals are about? Greeks?" another man asked his wife as she shook her head, not knowing. I knew from Michael that the murals were of ocean scenes and Poseidon; the god of the sea would be reigning over the main entrance. I remembered another argument we'd had, about men seemingly always getting the credit for things. As the wind blew across my face, I put all thoughts of the past out of my head and allowed myself to wonder where Michael was. Did he plan on attending tonight, or had he just wanted to make sure I didn't miss this?

"These murals were commissioned by the Wrigley family to welcome you to their magnificent island and this casino. They were designed by an artist on this very island, and his painstaking detail is visible in these stunning pieces. Michael Cathner was still putting his finishing touches on these this morning. He has worked tirelessly since last September to make sure they were nothing short of perfect for all of you tonight," the announcer continued. My mind went fuzzy. Michael designed the murals? *Fantastic, Gwen.*

One more thing I had criticized. Why hadn't he told me? "So, without further ado, Michael?"

The crowd clapped as Michael, dressed in a classic black tux, stepped up beside the announcer. My knees went weak. He looked…he looked gorgeous, the same as he always had. His eyes scanned the crowd as if he was searching for someone. I was standing several rows back when our eyes met. He smiled at me. I melted, and everyone else disappeared. The announcer cut back in with, "Ladies and gentlemen, we give you the murals!" Michael signaled the men behind him, who pulled large cords. With that, the silken panels dropped from the building, followed by oohs and ahhs.

I looked up; Michael was gone, and everyone moved toward the entrance, admiring the murals on their way in. I could only see one side panel from where I stood, but it was sensational—brightly colored coral and Garibaldi fish swimming through ribbons of kelp. *Michael, this is a masterpiece*, I thought, following the crowd around to the main entrance. Trying desperately not to step on my dress, I was looking down as we approached the entrance.

"Oh, Gwendolyn!" I heard Mary gasp, and then I looked up. The crowd filed into the main entrance, chattering, as I stood frozen, staring at the mural above. My face went flush, and if Simon had not been standing behind me I would have fainted. It was… it was indescribable. This was the most amazing gesture of love, strength, and passion I'd ever seen. It wasn't Poseidon, but a gorgeous mermaid, her body curved in an S, hands willowing to her sides. She was hovering over the entrance to the casino through purple strands of kelp, with sea life suspended below her. The mermaid's face was strong and serious while her body was alluring. Above her face floated her long, wavy auburn hair. The mermaid was powerful and commanding over all the other panels. She was perfect. I knew standing there she was the total embodiment of the way Michael saw me. *She is me. This is why he wanted me here. This is what he did with all of his heartache—he poured it into her.*

"Gwen, she looks a lot like—" Simon said, still supporting me from behind.

"I know," I cut in as a tear ran down my face. Everyone else had entered the casino. Simon and I could hear the orchestra in full force now.

"We should go in," he said.

"You go ahead. I need to stay here for a few minutes. I'll be right in." I smiled at Simon and nudged him toward the door.

"Don't be too long," he said, letting my hand drop as he walked into the casino.

# CHAPTER THIRTY-FIVE

Looking up at the way Michael saw me, I was overwhelmed by the love I felt for him and the way he loved me. This was nothing to be afraid of. I'd missed him so much, and in that moment I was ready. I wasn't sure if it was because of everything I'd been through since I left Catalina, but I was ready for him. He was already part of me. His love didn't eclipse me; it just made me more exquisite, like the mermaid. *Look at how strong and sensual she is. She's me on this island, with Michael.*

It was time to tell him everything I'd kept inside. He needed to know. Michael and I were the fairy tale. Far from perfect and often arguing, but my fairy tale. I'd been so wrong, and my father was right. I was hiding behind my mind, my judgments, and my theories. It was all in my head. Standing here in this beautiful dress, gorgeous and female, looking up at an image of myself, I'd never felt freer, less restricted, or more powerful. The tears rolled down my face.

"Of course, you had to outdo me tonight. Showing up looking even more incredible than the mural," Michael said, standing behind me.

I turned and saw him leaning up against a palm tree. He was smiling, tux jacket over one arm, taking all of me into his gaze. I wiped the tears from my cheeks and walked over to him. He met me halfway and stood staring into my eyes, his expression serious now.

"Do you like her?"

"Michael, she's…I mean, she looks like—"

"She is you, Gwen. She's everything I see when I look at you. She's smart and beautiful, stubborn and sensual. She commands respect, and everything clamors just to be near her. She's you, but seeing you here tonight, she pales in comparison. I—"

"What happened to Poseidon?" Only I would bring this up at a picture-perfect moment, but I wanted to know.

"You were right, and besides, I think everyone would much rather look up at you. I know I would." He smiled and I melted. Michael was so magnificent inside and out.

"She's breathtaking and…Thank you." My eyes welled up again.

Michael wiped my tears and whispered in my ear, "No, my love, thank you, for loving me—and for leaving me." He was holding my face, and I could not stop crying. "Most important, thank you for coming back to me. I love you, Gwen, and if you'll stay, I want to make a life with you, share a life with you. I want to see you every morning as my wife. Look around. We're everywhere on this island. It's where we fell in love and discovered each other. I'm so sorry, and I'll never again miss an opportunity to tell anyone and everyone, drunk or sober, how much I love you. You've rescued me from just existing. Please tell me it's not too late for us. Give me a chance to show you your fairy tale. No Mrs. Michael Cathner, I promise."

Now tears were welling up in his eyes. He put his head back and took a deep breath. Returning to my gaze, he said, "I've missed you so much. Please stay. Stay in my arms." With that, he pressed his lips over mine and kissed me softly. *I'd missed his touch.* Sliding one hand down my back, he carefully pulled me in toward his body. I breathed him into my heart. I was exactly where I belonged.

Everything had led me to this moment. My tears were a release of all the rules I'd placed on myself and all the pain I'd felt without Michael. Sharing a life, that's exactly what I wanted. It was such a simple idea, but it took strength to allow a person to be who they are and make them yours at the same time. We would tear down our walls one last time and never, ever rebuild. But before we could do any of this, there was one thing I needed to give him. The gift he already felt, but that I could never bring myself to say. The palms rustled in the wind above and my eyes opened.

"Rescued you? We've rescued each other. How's that for a fairy tale? I'm so sorry I hurt you." My face was streaked with tears. I felt cleansed. "Michael," I said, taking a very deep breath and looking into his beautiful face. I wanted to remember this moment forever. With everything I had, I said, "I love you. I always have. It took me a while to get here, to get to you, but I love you with my whole heart, and nothing, nothing will ever scare me again." His face was glowing. He looked so happy. Putting his lips close to mine, he said, "I love you, too," and kissed me again. Michael held my hand and led me under the mural and into the casino.

Just inside was a massive entry ramp. As we reached the first floor, we saw couples in the salon, lingering by a bar. Elegant men in tuxedos and women in the most beautiful gowns were everywhere. The entire space sparkled, and the hum of the even larger crowd above was enticing. We continued up the ramp and arrived at the entrance to the ballroom. Rich, warm rose hues filled the space, and through the arch in front of us was a huge, circular dance floor. We stood at the entrance, taking in the full grandeur of the casino with its glistening chandeliers and giant murals. If this was a fairy tale, we were in the perfect setting. Michael held my hand and talked a mile a minute, explaining the final months of construction. He was beaming just to have been part of such a masterpiece.

He walked me over to the bar, which stretched in an arch overlooking the dance floor. The mirror behind the bartender revealed hundreds of couples spinning in unison with the musicians, who were all dressed in white coats. Each couple with a unique story, one all their own, but tonight, in this ballroom, dancing together. As Michael paid for our drinks, I looked at the two of us in the foreground, a couple, with *our* unique story. I realized at that moment that everyone, no matter who they are, wants to feel this, their own fairy tale. *Some women want to be taken care of, and some men want to be caretakers. That is all right. There is someone for everyone, and no longer does everyone have to fit into the rigid categories I'd created in my youth. More and more, there are women who want something for themselves and men, like Michael, who see the wonder in that. There is no right answer. Every story stands alone as part of a grander picture.*

I turned to see my parents dancing. My mother was exquisite, and even at her age, was still the beautiful woman my father had fallen so in love with. Mary and George were seated in the glow of candlelight, talking and laughing. They were holding hands across a table, looking very much in love. Even Simon had a woman in his arms. I caught his eye as he went out toward the balcony to walk with his companion in the moonlight. He blew me a kiss and nodded to Michael. I had joined them in this sometimes risky dance of life. I was no longer safely on the sidelines. I'd jumped in and, in that process, found my own story.

"So, what do you think?" Michael asked. I was transported back to the tile factory, the first day I met Michael, when he'd asked me the same question. That day I was so full of myself, so flustered at being out of my element. I loved that girl, but at this moment I was quite proud of the woman I was becoming.

"What do I think? I think…I think I want to dance with you," I replied, smiling.

Michael laughed and quickly responded, "Why, Miss Ross, I thought you didn't dance. Dancing is for…what was it?"

"Me. Dancing with you, Mr. Cathner, is definitely for me. Now, do you want to dance with me or not?" We both laughed.

Michael kissed me and then led me out into the sea of other couples. Looking into his eyes, I knew that our life might get complicated. Our story, like that of many others on this dance floor, might have tough years, and more moments of pain, but I wasn't afraid. I knew, holding this man, my partner, in my arms, that no matter what came our way, our love, our friendship, and most of all our laughter would see us through.

ACKNOWLEDGMENTS

I would like to thank:

Catalina Island for years of wonderful memories.
The Catalina Island Conservancy for protecting and preserving such an incredible place to dream.
Paul Bagdon for reading, rereading, and always offering honest encouragement.
Avalon Books for "seeing" my story.

# ABOUT THE AUTHOR

Photo by EME Photography, 2012

Tracy Ewens was born in San Francisco and enjoys traveling to far-off places—both around the globe and in her mind. She believes TV is highly overrated and almost anything worth saying has come from either Anna Quindlen or Robert Fulghum. *Catalina Kiss* is her first novel. She lives with her husband and three children in New River, Arizona.

Made in the USA
Monee, IL
07 September 2026

62521474R00112